The Jealous Extremaduran

CERVANTES

THE JEALOUS
EXTREMADURAN

TRANSLATED BY C. A. JONES

PENGUIN BOOKS

PENGUIN BOOKS
Published by the Penguin Group
Penguin Books USA Inc., 375 Hudson Street,
New York, New York 10014, U.S.A.
Penguin Books Ltd, 27 Wrights Lane,
London W8 5TZ, England
Penguin Books Australia Ltd, Ringwood,
Victoria, Australia
Penguin Books Canada Ltd, 10 Alcorn Avenue,
Toronto, Ontario, Canada M4V 3B2
Penguin Books (N.Z.) Ltd, 182–190 Wairau Road,
Auckland 10, New Zealand

Penguin Books Ltd, Registered Offices:
Harmondsworth, Middlesex, England

Published in Penguin Books 1995

These stories are from *Exemplary Stories* by Miguel de Cervantes
Saavedra, translated by C. A. Jones, published by Penguin Books.

ISBN 0 14 60.0157 5

Printed in the United States of America

CONTENTS

The Jealous Extremaduran

Not many years ago a gentleman born of noble parents set out from a village in Extremadura, and like a second Prodigal Son went off through various parts of Spain, Italy and Flanders, wasting his time and his substance. After much wandering, his parents having died and his inheritance spent, he came to live in the great city of Seville, where he found plenty of opportunity to get through the little that he had left. So, seeing himself so short of money, and with few friends left, he had recourse to the solution to which many ruined people of that city are driven, namely that of going to the Indies, the refuge and shelter of all desperate folk in Spain, the sanctuary of bankrupts, the safe-conduct of murderers, the protection and cover of those gamblers known by the experts in the craft as sharpers, the general decoy for loose women, where many go to be deceived, and few find a way out of their difficulties. In short, when there was a fleet leaving for Tierrafirme, he came to terms with the commander, got together a store of provisions and an esparto mat; and embarking at Cadiz, and saying goodbye to Spain, he set off with the fleet. Amid general rejoicing the ship hoisted sail, and was carried off by a fair wind that soon took them out of sight of land and opened up to them the broad and ample plains of that great father of all waters, the Atlantic Ocean.

Our passenger was thoughtful, turning over in his memory the many and varied dangers which he had passed through in the years of his wandering, and the lack of direction which had characterized the whole of his life; and from his stock-taking he came to a firm decision to change his way of life and to adopt another manner of looking after whatever fortune God might be pleased to give him. He also determined to proceed with more caution towards women than hitherto. The fleet was almost becalmed when Filipo de Carrizales, which was the name of the man who is the subject of our story, was passing through this storm in his mind. The wind blew again, driving the ships on with such force that everyone was tossed hither and thither; and so Carrizales had to leave his ponderings and allow himself to be preoccupied simply by the problems of the voyage. This voyage was so successful that without suffering any set-back or shift in the wind they reached the port of Cartagena. And to cut out all the details which have nothing to do with our purpose, I should tell you that when Filipo went to the Indies he would be about forty-eight years old, and during the twenty he spent overseas, by his industry and diligence, he managed to make a hundred and fifty thousand good solid pesos.

So, seeing himself rich and prosperous, and feeling the natural desire which everyone has to return to his native land, he put off the important business he had in hand, and leaving Peru, where he had made such a rich harvest, he brought it all back to Spain in bars of gold and silver, in bond to save trouble. He landed in Sanlúcar; reached Seville, that ancient and wealthy city; collected his property without any trouble, looked up his friends, found them all dead, and decided to go off to his own part of the country, although he had already heard that death had not left him any of his relatives. If when he went off to the Indies, poor and in need, he had been assailed by many thoughts which did not leave him a moment's peace amid the waves of the sea, now in the calm of dry land they assailed him no less, although for different reasons. For whereas formerly he could not sleep because he was poor, now he could find no rest because he was rich; for wealth is just as heavy a burden for one who is not accustomed to bear it and does not know how to make use of it, as poverty is to one who is continually forced to endure it. Gold brings cares and so does the lack of it: but the cares of poverty are alleviated when one attains a moderate fortune, and those of wealth increase the more one gets.

Carrizales thought about his bars of gold and silver, not in any miserly way, because he had learned to be generous in his years as a soldier, but because he wondered what to do with them. To keep them in the form of bars was pointless, and to keep them at home was an incentive to the covetous and a stimulus to thieves. The urge to return to the restless life of a merchant had gone, and it seemed to him that in view of his age he had too much money. He wanted to spend his days in his own country and invest his property, passing his old age there in peace and quiet, giving to God what he could, since he had given to the world more than he should. At the same time, he thought that his homeland and the people in it were very poor, and that to go and live there would be to make himself the target of all the importunity to which the poor subject the rich man who is their neighbour, and especially when there is no one else in the village to run to with their troubles. He wanted someone to whom he could leave his possessions at the end of his days, and with this wish in mind he looked into the state of his health, and it seemed to him that he was still fit enough to get married. But at the thought of this he was so terrified that he felt like a mist driven by the wind. By nature he was the most jealous man in the world, even without being married; the mere thought of marrying was enough to arouse his jealousy, weary him with suspicions and startle him with imaginary evils, so much so that he resolved at all costs not to marry.

And having made up his mind about this, but not about what he was going to do with his life, fate determined that one day as he was going along a street he raised his eyes and saw a young girl at a window, who appeared to be thirteen or fourteen years old, so pleasant to look at and so beautiful, that, unable to help himself, good old Carrizales surrendered the weakness of his old age to the youth of Leonora, which was the name of the beautiful girl. And immediately he began to make endless speeches to himself, saying such things as:

'This girl is beautiful, and from the look of this house she can't be wealthy; she is only a girl; her youth may be sufficient to set my suspicions at rest. I shall marry her; I shall shut her up and train her in my ways, and so that she won't know anything else but what I shall teach her. I am not so old that I need lose hope of having children to be my heirs. There's no point in worrying about whether she has a dowry or not, since heaven has given me enough for our needs. Those who are rich have no need to look for property when they marry, but merely to find pleasure, for pleasure prolongs life, and the lack of it between married couples shortens it. Enough then, the die is cast, and this is the girl that heaven wishes me to have.'

And so some days later, when he had gone through this soliloquy not once but a hundred times, he spoke to Leonora's parents, and learned that, although poor, they were noble; and telling them of his intention and of his rank and fortune, he begged them to give him their daughter as his wife. They asked him for time to verify what he said, and so that he too would have time to find out whether what they had said about their nobility was true. They took leave of each other, investigated each other's credentials and found that what both said was true. So at last Leonora became Carrizales's wife, after he had given her a dowry of twenty thousand ducats, so fired was the heart of the jealous old man with love. He had scarcely taken his marriage vow when he was suddenly attacked by a raging jealousy, and without any reason began to tremble and to be more worried than he had ever been in his life. The first sign that he gave of his jealous condition was his unwillingness to let any tailor measure his wife for all the clothes which he wanted made for her; and so he went in search of another woman of more or less the same figure and size as Leonora's. He found a poor girl, and had a dress made to her measurements, and trying it on his wife, he found that it fitted her well. So, using the same measurements, he had the rest of the clothes made, in such quantity and quality that the parents of the girl couldn't believe their luck in having found such a good son-in-law, for their own sake and their daughter's. The girl was astonished at the sight of so much finery, because she had never in her life had more than a serge skirt and a taffeta cloak.

The second indication of jealousy that Filipo gave was in not wanting to live with his wife until he had set up a separate house for her, which he arranged in this way. He bought one costing twelve thousand ducats, in one of the best parts of the town, with running water and a garden with lots of orange-trees; he shut up all the windows facing on to the street, and opened up skylights all over the house. At the street entrance which is called the 'house door' in Seville, he had a stable built for a mule, and above it a straw loft and a room for the man who was to be in charge of it, who was an old Negro eunuch; he raised the walls above the level of the roofs so that anyone going into the house had to look straight up to the sky, without being able to see anything else; and he made a revolving door, which led from the house door to the patio. He bought rich furnishings to decorate the house, so that with its tapestries, furniture and canopies, it was obviously the property of a gentleman of means; he also purchased four slave girls, whom he branded on the face, as well as two newly-imported Negro girls. He made arrangements with a caterer to supply him with food, on condition that he did not sleep in the house nor come beyond the revolving door – through which he would have to hand the things he brought. When this was done, he leased some of his property in several of the best parts of the city; he put some of his money in the bank, and kept some for such contingencies as might arise. He also had a master key made for the whole house, and bought in season enough stores for the whole year. When he had arranged and set everything up in this fashion, he went to the house of his parents-in-law and asked for his wife, whom they handed over to him amid much weeping, because it seemed to them that she was being led off to her grave.

Poor Leonora did not know what had happened to her; and so, weeping with her parents, she asked for their blessing, and saying goodbye to them, surrounded by her slaves and maids and clutching her husband's hand, she came to her house, and when they were inside Carrizales delivered a sermon to all of them, instructing them to guard Leonora, and in no circumstances to let anyone come in beyond the second door, even the black eunuch. And the principal duty of guarding and looking after Leonora was entrusted to a wise and circumspect duenna, who was a sort of governess for Leonora, with the duty of supervising everything that went on in the house and overseeing the slaves and two other girls of the same age as Leonora, who had been brought in so that she should have the company of someone of her own age. He promised that he would treat and look after them in such a way that they would not regret their confinement, and that on saints' days they would all without exception go to hear Mass; but so early that the light of day would scarcely fall upon them. The servants and slaves promised him that they would do everything as he ordered, readily and willingly and without complaint; and the new bride, shrugging her shoulders, bowed her head and said that she had no will but that of her husband and master, to whom she would always be obedient.

When all these arrangements had been made and the good Extremaduran was settled in his house, he began to enjoy the fruits of marriage to the best of his ability, fruits which were neither pleasing nor disagreeable to Leonora, since she had no experience of any others; and so she spent her time with her duenna, her ladies-in-waiting and her slaves, while they found their enjoyment in eating sweetmeats; and rarely did a day pass without their making a hundred and one tasty things with honey and sugar. They had plenty of what was needed for this, and their master was very happy to give it to them, for he thought that they would be entertained and occupy their minds with all this and have no occasion to start thinking about their confinement. Leonora lived on terms of equality with her maids and took part in the same pleasures as they did, and in her innocence even started making dolls and other girlish things, which showed how simple-minded and childlike she was. All this was infinitely satisfying to the jealous husband, who thought that he had been happier in choosing his way of life than he could imagine, and that there was no way in which human ingenuity or malice could disturb his calm; so his only concern was to bring presents for his wife and remind her to ask him for anything that might occur

7

to her, promising that he would see that she got all that she wanted.

The days when she went to Mass, which was, as we've said, at first light, her parents would come too and would talk to their daughter in church in front of her husband, who gave them so many gifts that although they were sorry for their daughter, on account of the confinement in which she lived, they were consoled by the many presents which Carrizales, their generous son-in-law, gave them.

He would get up early in the morning, and wait for the arrival of the caterer, who was told the night before, by means of an order which they put in the revolving hatch, what he was to bring the following day; and when the caterer came, Carrizales would set off, usually on foot, leaving the two doors shut, the street door and the middle door, with the Negro stationed in between. He would attend to his affairs, which were not very considerable, and was soon back. Then, shutting himself up, he would spend his time giving presents to his wife and treats to the servants, who were all very fond of him, because he was so easy-going and pleasant, and especially because he was so generous to all of them. In this way they spent their novice year, and went on to make their profession in that way of life, resolving to continue in it to the end of their days. And this is how things would have turned out if that cunning disturber of the human race had not upset things, as you shall now hear.

Let him who thinks himself prudent and cautious tell me now what more precautions old Filipo could have taken, for he did not even allow any male animal in his house. The mice in it were never chased away by a male cat, nor was the bark of a dog ever heard there; they were all of the female sex. By day he would be thinking; by night he would lie awake, patrolling and guarding his house, the Argus of his loved one; and no man ever came inside the patio door, for he would do business with his friends in the street. The figures on the hangings in his halls and rooms were all females, or else flowers and woodland scenes. His whole house had an air of virtue and seclusion; even in the stories which the servants told in the long winter nights by the fireside, nothing lascivious was ever mentioned when he was present.

The silver of the old man's hair was pure gold to the eyes of Leonora, because the first love of a maiden makes an imprint on her soul like that of a seal on wax. The close custody in which she was kept seemed like sensible caution to her; she thought and believed that all recently married wives went through the same experience as she did. Her thoughts did not stray beyond the walls of her house, nor did she wish for anything but what her husband desired. Only on the days when she went to Mass did she see the streets, and this was so early in the morning that except on the way back from church there was not enough light even to see them properly. Never was monastery more enclosed, nor nuns more withdrawn, nor golden apples more strictly guarded; but for all this, it was impossible to avoid falling into the danger he feared; or at least, thinking that he had fallen into it.

There is in Seville a class of useless idle people usually known as men about town; these are the richer young men from every parish, lazy, showy, plausible people, about whose dress and manner of living, and whose customs and rules of conduct a good deal could be said; but we'll leave that aside for good reason. One of these fellows, known in their own jargon as a *virote*, a young bachelor – the ones who are recently married are called *mantones* – happened to look at the house of the cautious Carrizales, and seeing it always shut up, he was anxious to know who lived in it. He was so curious and so energetic in his inquiry, that he soon found out everything he wanted to know. He learned what the old man was like, of his wife's beauty and how he guarded her; all of which stimulated in turn the desire to see if it would be possible to storm, either by force or by cunning, such a well-guarded citadel. Discussing it with two *virotes* and a *mantón* who were friends of his, they agreed to set to work on it; for there is never a shortage of advisers and helpers for this sort of task.

The difficulty was to find out how to set about such a hazardous exercise; and having discussed it several times, they agreed on this plan: that Loaysa, as the *virote* was called, pretending that he was leaving the city for a few days, should keep out of sight of his friends. This he did. He then put on some clean drill trousers and a clean shirt, but on top he put clothes which were so torn and patched that there wasn't a poor man in the whole city who wore such vile things; he cut off his beard, put a patch over his eye, bound up one of his legs tightly, and supporting himself on crutches, transformed himself effectively into such a broken-down wreck that not even the most genuine cripple could rival him.

In this guise he would station himself every night at prayer time at the door of Carrizales's house, which was already closed, the Negro, who was called Luis, being shut up between the two doors. Standing there, Loaysa would take out a rather grimy guitar with a few strings missing, and as he was something of a musician, he would begin to strum a few gay and merry tunes, changing his voice so as not to be recognized. Then he would go on to sing some cheerful Moorish ballads so pleasantly and with such spirit that everyone who went along the street would stop to listen to him, and always, as soon as he started singing, he would find himself surrounded by children. The Negro Luis, listening from his position between the doors, was spellbound by the *virote*'s music, and would have given his right arm to be able to open the door, and listen more easily; so strong is the love which Negroes have for music. And when Loaysa wanted those who were listening to him to leave him, he would stop singing, pick up his guitar and, taking up his crutches, would be off.

He had performed four or five times for the Negro – for it was merely for his sake that he did it, as it seemed to him that the way to begin the demolition of that edifice was and must be through the Negro – and his plans were not in vain, because one night, going up to the door as usual, he began to tune his guitar, and realized that the Negro was already waiting for him. So, going to the crack at the side of the door, he said softly,

'Do you think, Luis, that you could give me a drop of water, for I'm dying of thirst and I can't sing?'

'No,' said the Negro, 'for I haven't got the key to this door, and there's no hole through which I could give it to you.'

'But who has the key?' asked Loaysa.

'My master,' answered the Negro, 'who is the most jealous man in the world. And if he knew that I was talking to someone here and now, that would be the end of me. But who are you, asking me for water?'

'I'm a poor man with a lame leg,' answered Loaysa, 'and I earn my living begging from good folk in the name of God; and as well as this I am teaching some Negroes and other poor people to play. I've already got three Negroes, slaves of three of the city aldermen, whom I've taught so that they can sing and play

11

at any dance and in any inn, and they've paid me very well indeed for it.'

'I'd pay you a good deal better,' said Luis, 'if I had the chance to take lessons; but it's impossible, because when my master goes out in the morning, he closes the street door, and when he comes back he does the same, leaving me shut up between the two doors.'

'By Jove, Luis,' replied Loaysa, who already knew the Negro's name, 'if you could find a way for me to get in at night now and then, in less than a fortnight I'd have you so expert at the guitar that you could play on any street corner without embarrassment; because I assure you I am a very skilful teacher. Moreover, I've heard that you are very talented, and from what I can judge by the sound of your voice, which is rather high-pitched, you must sing very well.'

'I don't sing too badly,' answered the Negro; 'but what's the use if I don't know a single tune except the one about the Star of Venus, and the one that goes:

> By a green meadow . . .

and that one that's in fashion just now, which goes:

> With my trembling hand clutching
> The bars of a window.'

'Those are trifles,' said Loaysa, 'compared with the ones I could teach you, because I know all the ones about the Moor Abindarráez, the ones about his lady Jarifa, all the ones they sing about the story of the great Sufi Tuman-Bey; and the ones that go with the sacred version of the saraband, which are so marvellous that they even make the Portuguese sit up and take notice. I teach all this by such easy methods, that even if you're

12

in no hurry to learn, by the time you've eaten three or four pecks of salt you'll be a fluent performer on every kind of guitar.'

At this the Negro sighed and said, 'What is the use of all this, if I can't get you into the house?'

'I have the answer,' said Loaysa. 'You try to take the keys from your master, and I will give you a piece of wax, on which you can take the imprint in such a way that the wards are marked on the wax; and as I've become rather fond of you, I'll get a locksmith who's a friend of mine to make the keys, and so I'll be able to get in at night and teach you better than Prester John of the Indies. I think it's a great pity that a voice like yours should be wasted, simply for lack of support from the guitar; for you should know, brother Luis, that the best voice in the world goes off when it is not accompanied by an instrument, be it guitar or clavichord, organ or harp; but the one which most suits your voice is the guitar, being the easiest and least costly instrument.'

'This seems fine to me,' replied the Negro, 'but it can't be done, because the keys never come into my possession. My master never lets them out of his hands during the day, and at night they're kept under his pillow when he's asleep.'

'Then think of something else, Luis,' said Loaysa, 'if you're keen to be an accomplished musician; for if you're not, it's not worth my taking the trouble to give you advice.'

'What do you mean, if I'm keen?' replied Luis. 'I'm so keen that there's nothing humanly possible that I won't do, in order to learn music.'

'Well, if that's so,' said the *virote*, 'I'll pass you some pincers and a hammer, if you will make room by taking away some of the earth by the hinge; and with them you'll be able to take the nails out of the lock very easily, and then just as easily we shall put back the plate so that no one can see that the nails have been taken out. Once I am inside, shut up with you in your loft or wherever you sleep, I'll be so quick doing what I have to do, that you'll see even more than I've told you, to my advantage and your satisfaction. And don't worry about what we shall have to eat: I'll bring enough supplies to last both of us a week, for I've pupils and friends who will see to it that I come to no harm.'

'As far as food is concerned,' replied the Negro, 'there'll be no cause for worry; for with the ration I get from my master and the leftovers I get from the slave girls there'll be plenty of food for two more people. Let's have this hammer and pincers you talk about, and I'll make room under the door by the hinge for you to pass it through, and then cover it up and seal it with mud; for even if I have to tap once or twice taking off the plate, my master sleeps so far from this door that it'll be a miracle, or hard luck on our part, if he hears it.'

'Then to work,' said Loaysa; 'for in two days from now, Luis, you will have all you need to carry out our plan; and take care not to eat things that cause phlegm, because they do more harm than good to your voice.'

'Nothing makes me more hoarse than wine,' answered the Negro, 'but I shan't give that up for all the voices on earth.'

'That's not what I mean,' said Loaysa. 'God forbid. Drink, Luis my boy, drink and much good may it do you, for wine drunk in moderation never did anyone any harm.'

'I do drink in moderation,' replied the Negro. 'I have a jug here which contains exactly two litres; the slaves fill this for me without my master knowing, and the caterer secretly brings me a little wineskin, which contains exactly four litres and which fills this up when it runs out.'

'That's excellent,' said Loaysa, 'for a dry throat can neither grunt nor sing.'

'God be with you,' said the Negro; 'but see that you don't fail to come here at night to sing while you're looking for the things you need to get in here, for my fingers are itching to have a go at the guitar.'

'You bet I'll come,' replied Loaysa. 'And what's more I'll bring new songs.'

'That's what I want,' said Luis; 'and now don't go without singing something for me, so that I may go happily to bed; and as far as payment is concerned, you may be sure, my poor sir, that I'll pay you better than any rich man.'

'I'm not concerned about that,' said Loaysa, 'for you can pay me as I teach you. For the moment listen to this little tune, and when I get inside you'll see wonders.'

'Splendid,' answered the Negro.

When this long conversation was over, Loaysa sang a brisk little ballad, with which he left the Negro happy and satisfied and hardly able to wait to open the door.

Loaysa had scarcely left the door when, more swiftly than you'd expect in view of his crutches, he went to tell his advisers of the good beginning he had made, an earnest of the good ending which he expected. He found them and told them what he had agreed with the Negro. The next day they found the instruments, so effective that they could break any nail as easily as if it were made of wood.

The *virote* did not fail to go and entertain the Negro with music again, nor did the Negro neglect to make the hole for the things his teacher was going to give him, covering it in such a way that if one weren't deliberately looking one would never realize there was a hole there. The second night Loaysa gave him the instruments, and Luis tried his strength, and almost without any effort found himself with the nails broken and the plate of the lock in his hands. He opened the door and welcomed his teacher inside like Orpheus himself. When he saw him with his two crutches and so ragged, with his leg all bandaged up, he was amazed. Loaysa wasn't wearing the patch over his eye, as it wasn't necessary, and as soon as he got in, he embraced his good pupil and kissed him on the face, and then put a big wineskin in his hands and a box of preserves and other sweetmeats, of which he had a good supply. And putting aside his crutches, as if there were nothing wrong with him, he began to caper about. The Negro was so surprised at this that Loaysa said to him:

'You must know, brother Luis, that my lameness and broken-down appearance are not the result of any affliction, but are contrived as a means of earning my food, begging for the love of God; and with the help of this and of my music, I have the best time in the world – a world in which all those who are not clever and scheming will die of hunger, as you will see in the course of our friendship.'

'Time will tell,' answered the Negro, 'but let's set about putting this plate back, so that no one can see what's been done to it.'

'Right ho,' said Loaysa.

He took some nails out of his bag and they fixed the lock so that it was as good as before, which delighted the Negro. Loaysa went up to the room in the loft, and settled down as best he could. Luis lit a taper, and without further ado, Loaysa took out his guitar, and playing softly he left the poor Negro quite carried away as he listened to it. After he had played a little, he took some food out again and gave it to his pupil, who drank

16

with such a will from the wineskin that he was more carried away by the wine than the music. After this, he started Luis on his lesson; but as the poor Negro had a good load of wine on board, he couldn't get a note right. All the same Loaysa made him believe that he knew at least two tunes, and the funny thing was that the Negro swallowed it, and spent the whole night strumming the guitar out of tune and without touching the right strings.

They slept for what little of the night was left, and about six in the morning Carrizales came down and opened the middle door, and the street door also, and stood waiting for the caterer, who came shortly afterwards, and putting the food through the revolving door, went off again. Then he called to the Negro to come down and take the barley for the mule, and his own ration of food. When Luis had taken it, old Carrizales went off, leaving both doors shut, without seeing what had been done to the street door, at which both master and pupil were not a little pleased.

The master had barely left the house when the Negro grabbed the guitar and began to play so loudly that all the servants heard him and asked him through the revolving door,

'What is this, Luis? How long have you had a guitar, and who gave it to you?'

'Who gave it to me?' said Luis. 'The best musician in the world, and one who is going to teach me more than six thousand notes in less than six days.'

'And where is this musician?' asked the duenna.

'Not very far from here,' answered the Negro, 'and if it weren't that I'm embarrassed and afraid of my master, I might show him to you now, and I promise you'd be delighted to see him.'

'And where can he be for us to see him,' asked the duenna, 'if no man but our master has ever entered this house?'

'Well,' said the Negro, 'I don't want to say anything to you until you see what I know and what he has taught me in the short time I've said.'

'Certainly,' said the duenna, 'unless it's some devil who's going to teach you, I don't know who can make a musician out of you in such a short time.'

'You wait,' said the Negro, 'and you'll hear and see one of these days.'

'It's impossible,' said one of the maids, 'for we have no windows looking on to the street to be able to see or hear anyone.'

'That's all right,' said the Negro; 'for while there's life there's hope: and especially if you can and will keep quiet.'

'You bet we'll keep quiet, brother Luis,' said one of the slave girls. 'We'll be more quiet than if we were dumb; because I promise you, my friend, I'm dying to hear a good voice, for since we've been walled up here, we haven't even heard the birds singing.'

Loaysa was listening to all this conversation with great satisfaction, thinking that it was all directed towards the attainment of his ends, and that good fortune had been with him in guiding the conversation according to his wishes. The servants went off with a promise from the Negro that when they least expected it he would call them to listen to a very good voice, then, fearing that his master would return and find him talking to them, he left them and withdrew to his retreat. He would have liked to carry on with his lessons, but he did not dare to play during the day, lest his master should hear him. Carrizales came shortly afterwards, and closing the doors as his custom was, he shut himself up in the house. Luis told the Negress who happened to give him his food that night, that they should all come down to the hatch after his master had gone to sleep and that they would hear the voice without fail as he had promised them. It is true that before he said this he had begged his teacher earnestly to be so kind as to sing and play at the revolving door that night, so that he could keep the promise he had made to the maids that they should hear a remarkable voice, and assured him that he would be extremely well treated by all of them. The teacher pretended to be reluctant to do what he in fact most wanted to do; but finally he said that he would do what his good pupil asked, simply to give him pleasure. The Negro embraced him and gave him a kiss on the cheek, to show how pleased he was at this promised favour; and that day he fed Loaysa as well as if he had been eating in his own home, and perhaps even better, for he might well have been short of something there.

Night came, and at midnight or just before there were whisperings at the revolving door, and Luis realized that it was the crowd of servants coming. So he called his teacher and they came down from the loft, with the guitar well strung and tuned. Luis asked who and how many were listening. They replied that they were all there except their mistress, who was sleeping with her husband. Loaysa was sorry about this, but all the same, he wanted to get his plan under way and give pleasure to his pupil; so playing the guitar softly, he made such beautiful sounds that the Negro was amazed and the flock of women who were listening to him astounded. What shall I say about their feelings when they heard him play 'Woe is me' and finish up with the lively sound of the saraband, new to Spain at that time? Every one of the older women was dancing, and the young ones were beside themselves, although they all kept remarkably quiet, with guards and spies posted to give warning if the old man should wake. Loaysa also sang *seguidillas*, with which he filled to overflowing the cup of pleasure of the listeners, who pestered the Negro to tell them who this marvellous musician was. The Negro told them that he was a poor beggar, the nicest and finest-looking man you could find among all the beggars in Seville. They pleaded with him to arrange for them to see him, and not to let him leave the house for at least a fortnight, for they would look after him very well and give him everything he needed. They asked him how he had managed to get him into the house. He didn't say a word in answer to this; all he would say was that if they wanted to see him they should make a little hole in the revolving door which they could stop up with wax afterwards; and that as far as keeping him in the house was concerned, he would see what he could do.

Loaysa also spoke to them, putting himself at their service, and with such convincing arguments that they realized they were beyond the intelligence of a poor beggar. They asked him to come to the same place the following night, and said they would arrange with their mistress that she should come down and listen to him, although their master was a light sleeper, not because of his great age, but because of his great jealousy. To this Loaysa said that if they wanted to hear him without upsetting the old man he would give them some powder to put in his wine to make him sleep more heavily and for longer than usual.

'Heaven help us!' said one of the ladies. 'If this were true, what good fortune would have come to us unexpected and undeserved. It wouldn't be sleeping powder for him so much as life-giving powder for all of us and for my poor mistress Leonora his wife, for he doesn't leave her day or night and doesn't let her out of his sight for a single moment. Oh, sir, bring this

20

powder and may God give you all the blessings you desire! Be off, and don't be long; bring it, sir, for I'll be happy to mix it with the wine and act as butler; and God grant that the old man sleeps for three days and nights, which would be heaven for us.'

'Well, I'll bring it,' said Loaysa, 'and it won't do any harm to anyone who takes it apart from making him sleep very heavily.'

They all begged him to bring it quickly, and having agreed to make a hole in the revolving door with a gimlet the next night, and to bring their mistress to see and hear him, they went off. Although it was almost day, the Negro wanted to have his lesson, which Loaysa gave him, giving him to understand that not one of all his pupils had a better ear than he, when in fact the poor Negro didn't know, and never learned, how to play a note.

Loaysa's friends took care to come at night to listen at the street doors, to see if their friend had anything to say to them or if he needed anything. Giving a signal which they had agreed on, Loaysa found that they were at the door, and through the gap by the hinge he told them briefly of the good state in which affairs stood. He asked them earnestly to look for something to give to Carrizales which would induce sleep, for he had heard that there was a powder which did this. They told him they had a friend who was a doctor, who would give them the best thing he knew, if there was any to be had; and urging him to carry on with the plan, and promising to return the following night, with all caution and speed they left.

Night came, and the flock of doves came to the lure of the guitar. With them came innocent Leonora, fearful and trembling at the thought of her husband waking. Alarmed by this fear, she had not wished to come, but her servants, especially the duenna, said so many things to her about the soft tones of the music and the noble nature of the poor musician – for without having seen him she praised him and lauded him more highly than Absalom and Orpheus – that the poor lady, convinced and persuaded by them, was forced to do what she never wished or ever would wish to do. The first thing they did was to bore a hole in the revolving door to see the musician, who was no longer dressed as a poor beggar, but with breeches of tawny-coloured taffeta, full-cut like a sailor's; a doublet of the same stuff with gold braid, and a velvet cap of the same colour, with a starched collar with long points and lace on it; for he had brought all this with him in his knapsack, having an idea that the opportunity would come for him to change his clothes.

He was young, elegant and good-looking; and as all the ladies had been used to looking at their old master for such a long time, they thought they were seeing an angel. One would go up to the hole to look at him, then another, and so that they could see him better, the Negro moved the lighted taper up and down in front of him. And when they had all seen him, even the Negro slave girls, Loaysa took the guitar, and sang so exquisitely that night that they were all quite carried away, the old women and the girls alike. They all asked Luis to arrange for the teacher to come inside, so that they could hear and see him at close quarters, and not as if they were looking through a sextant; and moreover without being so dangerously far from their master, who could catch them suddenly and with the goods on them, which would not happen if they had him hidden inside.

Their mistress opposed this vigorously, saying that this must not happen and that he must not come in, because she would be very upset, and they could see and hear him safely from there, without danger to their honour.

'What honour?' said the duenna. 'The king has enough of that. You stay shut up with your Methuselah, and let us enjoy ourselves as best we can. Anyway, this gentleman seems so honourable that he won't want anything from us that we don't want to give him.'

'My ladies,' said Loaysa at this point, 'I came here simply to serve you with all my heart and soul, moved by your extraordinary isolation, and by the thought of the time you have to waste in this confined existence. Indeed, I am such a simple, inoffensive and good-tempered man, so compliant, that I shall do nothing but what I am told; and if any of you should say, "Maestro, sit here," "Maestro, go over there," "Lie down here," "Come over here," I'd do it like a tame dog doing its tricks.'

'If this is so,' said poor, ignorant Leonora, 'how shall we arrange for you to get in here?'

'Well,' said Loaysa, 'you do your best to make a wax copy of the key of this middle door, and I'll arrange to get another made which we can use tomorrow night.'

'When you've copied that key,' said one of the ladies, 'you've copied every one in the house, because it's a master key.'

'That's all to the good,' replied Loaysa.

'It's true,' said Leonora, 'but this gentleman must first swear that all he will do when he gets in here is sing and play when he's asked, and that he'll stay shut up and quiet wherever we put him.'

'I'll swear that,' said Loaysa.

'That oath is worthless,' answered Leonora. 'You must swear by the life of your father, and on the Cross, kissing it so that all of us may see.'

'By my father's life I swear,' said Loaysa; 'and by this sign of the Cross, which I kiss with my unclean mouth.'

And making a cross with two fingers, he kissed it three times. When he had done this, another of the ladies said, 'See that you don't forget about the powder, sir, for that's absolutely essential.'

With that the conversation ended for the night, everybody being very happy about the arrangement. And fortune, which was leading Loaysa's affair to a happy solution, just at that time, which was two o'clock in the morning, brought his friends along the street. They made the usual sign, which was to play a jew's harp, and Loaysa told them how things were, and asked them if they had brought the powder or something similar, as he had asked, to make Carrizales sleep; he also told them about the master key. They told him that the powder, or an ointment, would arrive the following night, so effective that, when the wrists and temples had been rubbed with it, it would induce a deep sleep, from which one would not awaken for two days unless one were bathed with vinegar in all the places where the ointment had been applied. They also asked him for the wax copy of the key, which they'd have made quite easily. With this they went off, and Loaysa longed for the next night to arrive, to see if they kept the promise about the key. And although time seems slow and dull to those who are waiting, in the end it catches up with one's thoughts and the desired end comes, for time never stands still.

So night came and with it the time at which they usually went to the revolving door, where all the house servants came, young and old, black and white, because they all wanted to see the musician in their seraglio. But Leonora did not come, and when Loaysa asked about her they replied that she was in bed with her husband, who had locked the door of the room where they slept, and after shutting it put the key under his pillow. They said that their mistress had told them that when the old man fell asleep she would try to take the master key from him and make a copy in wax, which she had made soft and ready; and that very shortly they were to go and get it through a cat's hole.

Loaysa was amazed at the old man's caution, but he did not lose heart nor his desire. At this point he heard the jew's harp so he went to the door and found his friends, who gave him a little jar of ointment of the sort they had described. Loaysa took it and told them to wait a little, and he would give them the master key. He went back to the revolving door and told the duenna, who was the one who most obviously wanted him to get in, to take it to her mistress Leonora, telling her how it worked and to try to rub it on her husband so that he didn't feel it, and that she would be amazed at what would happen. The duenna did this, and when she got to the hole, she found that Leonora was waiting for her lying flat on the floor, with her ear beside the hole. The duenna went up to it, and lying down in the same way, she put her lips to her mistress's ear, and whispered to her that she had the ointment and told her how she was to make it do its work. She took the ointment, and told her that it was quite impossible for her to take the key from her husband, as he hadn't put it under the pillow, as usual, but between the two mattresses and almost under the middle of his body; but told her to tell the teacher that if the ointment worked as he said, they would easily get the key whenever they wanted, so it wouldn't be necessary to make a wax copy of it. She told her to go and tell him immediately, and to come back to see if the ointment worked, because she intended to rub it on her husband straight away.

The duenna came down to tell Loaysa, and he sent away his friends, who were waiting for the key. Trembling and very gently, almost without daring to breathe, Leonora rubbed the ointment on the wrists of her jealous husband, and then on his nostrils. When she got to these she thought he shuddered and she was terrified, thinking she had been caught red-handed. But she finished rubbing the ointment as best she could in all the places which they told her were necessary, just as if she were embalming him for burial.

The opiate soon proved its effectiveness, because the old man straight away began to snore so loudly that he could be heard in the street, which was music more tuneful to the ear of his wife than that which the teacher played for the Negro. Still doubting her eyes, she went up to him and shook him a little, and then a bit more, and then a little more again, to see if he awoke; then she was so daring that she moved him about without his waking up. When she saw this, she went to the hole in the door, and not quite so softly as before, she called the duenna, who was waiting for her there, and said to her,

'Wonderful news, sister, Carrizales is sleeping like a corpse.'

'Then what are you waiting for to take the key, madam?' said the duenna. 'The musician has been waiting for it for more than an hour.'

'Wait, sister. I'll go and get it,' answered Leonora.

She went back to the bed, put her hand between the mattresses and took out the key without the old man's feeling it; and taking it in her hands, she began to jump for joy, and without more ado opened the door and handed it to the duenna, who received it with great delight. Leonora ordered her to go and open the door for the musician and bring him into the gallery, because she did not dare to move from there, for fear of what might happen; but first of all she insisted on his repeating the oath he had sworn, not to do anything but what they ordered; and that if he did not want to confirm his oath, they should not open the door to him on any account.

'I'll do that,' said the duenna, 'and indeed he shan't come in unless he swears and double-swears and kisses the Cross six times.'

'Don't be too rigid,' said Leonora. 'Let him kiss it as many times as he likes; but see that he swears by his father's and his mother's lives, and by everything he loves best, because then we shall be sure, and we'll hear him sing and play to our hearts' content, for indeed he does it beautifully. Now go on, and don't delay any longer, for we don't want to spend the night talking.'

The good duenna picked up her skirts, and rushed as fast as she could to the revolving door, where all the people in the house were waiting for her. When she had shown them the key she was carrying, they were so delighted that they lifted her shoulder high, like a professor, and shouted, 'Hurrah, hurrah!'; and even more so when she said there was no need to copy the key, because the old man was sleeping so soundly under the influence of the ointment that they could use the house key as often as they liked.

'Come on then, old friend,' said one of the ladies. 'Open the door and let this gentleman come in, for he's been waiting a long time, and let's have a bit of music without further delay.'

'But there must be further delay,' replied the duenna; 'for we have to make him swear an oath, like the other night.'

'He's so good,' said one of the slave girls, 'that he won't bother with oaths.'

The duenna then opened the door, and holding it ajar she called Loaysa, who had been listening to the whole thing through the hole in the revolving door. When he got up to the door, he wanted to come straight in, but the duenna put her hand on his chest, and said to him:

'You must know, sir, that by God and my conscience all of

us in this house are virgins like the mothers who bore us, except my lady; and although I must look forty, when I'm two and a half months short of thirty, I am one too, for my sins; and if by any chance I look old, it's because all the upsets, the work and the hardships put years on you. And this being so, it would not be right that in exchange for listening to two or three or four songs, we should lose all this virginity that's shut up here; because even this Negress, who's called Guiomar, is a virgin. So, my dear sir, before you come into our domain, you must swear a very solemn oath that you will do nothing but what we command; and if you think this is a lot to ask, bear in mind that a lot more is being risked. If you come with good intentions you won't much mind swearing; for a good payer doesn't mind giving pledges.'

'Señora Marialonso is right, absolutely right,' said one of the ladies, 'as you would expect from one who is so discreet and *comme il faut*; and if the gentleman does not wish to swear, let him not come in here.'

Whereupon the Negress Guiomar, who wasn't very good at the language, said, 'For me, swear or not swear, let him come in and all devil too; for although he swear if you are here he forget all about it.'

Loaysa listened very calmly to Marialonso's harangue, and gravely and solemnly he answered as follows:

'Certainly, my sisters and companions, my intention never was and never will be any other than that of giving you pleasure and happiness in everything that is in my power, and so I shan't make heavy weather of this oath which you are asking me to swear. But I should like you to put some trust in my word, because the word of a person like me is equivalent to entering into a binding contract; for I want you to know that under the sackcloth there is something of substance, and that beneath a poor cloak there is usually a good drinker. But so that you may all be sure of my good intentions, I am resolved to swear as a Catholic and as a man of honour; and so I swear solemnly by the immaculate virtue and by the passes of the holy mountain of Lebanon, and by everything in the preface to the true history of Charlemagne, including the death of the giant Fierabras, never to depart from the oath I have sworn and from the command of the least and humblest of these ladies, the penalty being that if I should do or wish to do otherwise, from now henceforward and thenceforward till now I declare it to be null and of no effect or validity.'

Our good Loaysa got to this point in his oath, when one of the ladies, who had been listening attentively to him, shouted out:

'This is indeed an oath to move the very stones! God forbid that I should want you to swear any more, for with what you've sworn already you could go into the Cave of Cabra itself!'

And grasping him by the breeches she dragged him in, and then all the rest made a circle round him. Then one of them went to give the news to her mistress, who was standing guard over her sleeping husband; and when the messenger told her that the musician was on his way up, she was delighted and upset at the same time and asked if he had sworn the oath. She answered that he had, and using the most novel form of oath she had ever come across in her life.

'Then if he has sworn,' said Leonora, 'we've got him. How wise I was to make him swear!'

At this point the whole crowd arrived together with the musician in the middle of them, and the Negro and the Negress Guiomar lighting them on their way. And when Loaysa saw

Leonora, he made as if to throw himself at her feet and to kiss her hands. She silently motioned him to get up, and they all kept their mouths shut, not daring to say a word lest their master should hear them. When Loaysa saw this, he told them that they could talk aloud without fear, for the ointment with which their master had been anointed was so powerful that, without actually taking his life away, it made a man seem just like a corpse.

'I can believe that,' said Leonora; 'for if it weren't so he would have woken up twenty times, so lightly does he sleep because of his many ailments; but since I rubbed the ointment on him, he's snoring like a beast.'

'Well, in that case,' said the duenna, 'let's go to that room opposite where we can hear the gentleman sing, and enjoy ourselves a bit.'

'Let's go,' said Leonora, 'but let Guiomar stay here on guard, so that she can tell us if Carrizales wakes up.'

To which Guiomar answered, 'I, black girl, stay; white girls go; God forgive us all.'

The Negress stayed behind, they went off to the drawing-room where there was a splendid dais, and placing the gentleman in the centre of it, they all sat down. And the good Marialonso took a candle, and began to look at the handsome musician from head to foot, and one said, 'What a splendid crop of hair he has, so handsome and curly!' Another said, 'Oh, what white teeth! You'd never find pine-kernels more white or more beautiful!' Another said, 'What eyes, so full and clear! And look how green they are, just like emeralds!' This one praised his mouth, that one his feet, and the whole lot of them together made a detailed study of him. Only Leonora was silent, and looked at him, and thought he was a finer-looking man than her husband. Thereupon the duenna took the guitar from the Negro, and put it in Loaysa's hands, begging him to play it and to sing some verses which were very popular in Seville at the time, and which went: 'Oh Mother, my mother, don't guard me so close.'

Loaysa did as she requested. They all got up and began to dance for all they were worth. The duenna knew the verses, and sang them with more vigour than talent, and they went like this:

> Oh Mother, my mother,
> don't guard me so close.
> I'll guard my own honour
> in the way I shall choose.
>
> They say it is written,
> well written I say,
> that privation well may
> cause men to be smitten,
> and girls to be bitten
> by a deep-hidden love.
> If it's true then I move
> that you no more time lose.
> I'll guard my own honour, etc.
>
> If a maiden's own will
> will not keep her from harm,
> fear'll not safeguard her charm,
> rank no virtue instil.
> The desire to fulfil
> it will break down all walls:
> death itself ne'er appals
> when love asks its dues.
> I'll guard my own honour, etc.
>
> The girl who is ready
> to fall victim to love,
> like a moth round a stove
> will hover unsteady,

for love's air is heady.
However well guarded,
your pains ill rewarded
I shall have to refuse.
I'll guard my own honour, etc.

Love's so strong in its power
that the most beauteous maid,
when its force is displayed,
will tremble and cower.
Her heart's soft as flour;
her desire's fierce heat
makes her hands and her feet
all their functions refuse.
I'll guard my own honour
in the way I shall choose.

The circle of girls, led by the good duenna, got to the end of their song and dance, when Guiomar, who was on guard, came up in great confusion, shaking as if she had a fit, and in a low hoarse voice, said, 'Master's awake, lady; and lady, master's awake, and get up and comes.'

If you've ever seen the way a flock of pigeons in a field calmly eating what others have sown fly up when suddenly disturbed by the angry sound of a gunshot, and wing their way through the air in confusion and astonishment, forgetting their food, you can imagine how the circle of dancers was left in terror and alarm, when they heard the unexpected news that Guiomar had brought. Each one looked for an excuse and they all tried to find a way of escape, one here, one there, rushing off to hide in the attics and corners of the house, leaving the musician alone. He, abandoning his guitar and his singing, was so alarmed that he did not know what to do. Leonora wrung her beautiful hands;

the lady Marialonso clapped her hands to her face, although not too hard; in short all was confusion, terror and alarm. But the duenna, being more shrewd and self-controlled, gave orders that Loaysa should go into one of her rooms, and that she and her mistress would stay in the hall for there would be no difficulty in finding an excuse to give to her master if he found them there.

Loaysa hid himself immediately, and the duenna listened carefully to see if her master was coming. Not hearing any noise, her courage returned, and gradually, a step at a time, she went along to the room where her master was sleeping. She heard him snoring just as he had been earlier; so, being reassured that he was sleeping, she picked up her skirts and came running back to tell her mistress the good news, news which she was only too happy to hear.

The good duenna did not wish to lose the opportunity which fortune offered her of enjoying before anyone else the charms which she imagined the musician possessed; and so, telling Leonora to wait in the hall until she came to call her, she left her and went into the room where he was waiting, his thoughts in a turmoil, for news of what the old man was doing. He cursed the unreliability of the ointment, and complained of the credulity of his friends and his own lack of forethought in not trying it on someone else before he used it on Carrizales. Just then the duenna came in, and assured him that the old man was sleeping like a log. He calmed down and listened to the loving words that Marialonso addressed to him, from which he deduced her evil intentions, deciding that he would use her as a hook to catch her mistress. And as they were both talking, the other servants who were hidden in various parts of the house, one here and one there, came back to see if it was true that their master had awakened. Seeing that everything was plunged in silence, they got as far as the hall where they had left their mistress, from whom they learned that their master was still asleep; and when they asked her about the musician and the duenna, she told them where they were, and they all went, as silently as they had come, to the hall, to listen at the door to what the two were talking about.

Among the gathering was the Negress Guiomar, but not the Negro, because as soon as he heard that his master had awakened, he clutched his guitar and went to hide in his loft, and taking cover under the blankets on his miserable bed, lay sweating with fear; yet he could not resist trying the strings of the guitar, so fond was the poor devil of music. The girls heard the old woman flirting with the musician, and they all started to curse her, calling her a witch and a hairy, bad-tempered old hag, and other things which out of respect we won't repeat; but what made everybody laugh more than anything were the things that the Negress Guiomar said. Being Portuguese and not very good at the language, the way she cursed the duenna was extraordinarily funny. In fact, the upshot of the conversation between the two was that he would fall in with her wishes if she first of all handed over her mistress completely to do with her as he wished.

The duenna was hard put to it to offer what the musician asked, but in return for satisfying the desire which had already taken possession of her body and soul, she promised him the most impossible things imaginable. She left him and went off to talk to her mistress. When she saw that all the servants crowded round her door, she told them to go to their rooms, for there would be a chance the next night to enjoy the musician's company without all this fuss: that night all the disturbance had taken away their pleasure.

They all understood quite well that the old woman wanted

to be left alone; yet they had to obey her, because she was in charge of them all. The servants went off, and she hurried off to the hall to persuade Leonora to accede to Loaysa's wishes, with such a long and well-argued harangue, that it looked as if she'd had it worked out for days. She praised his politeness, his bravery, his wit and his many charms; she pointed out to her how much more pleasing would be the embraces of the young lover than those of the old husband, assuring her that she could enjoy her pleasure in secret for as long as she liked, with other arguments of the same kind, which the devil put into her mouth, so persuasive, convincing and effective that they would have moved not only the tender and innocent heart of simple Leonora, but even a marble statue. Oh you duennas, placed by birth and custom in the world to bring to naught a thousand good honest intentions! You with your long, pleated head-dresses, chosen to rule over the halls and drawing-rooms of illustrious ladies, how ill you exercise your function, a function which is now more or less unavoidable! In short, the duenna said so much, the duenna was so persuasive, that Leonora gave in, Leonora was deceived and Leonora was ruined, putting an end to all the precautions of wise old Carrizales, who was sleeping like the corpse of his own honour.

Marialonso took her mistress by the hand, and almost by force, she led Leonora, her eyes swollen with tears, to where Loaysa was. Having given them her blessing with a devilish laugh, she closed the door after her and left them shut up there, while she went off to sleep in the drawing-room. Rather, she went to wait for her reward, but exhausted after so many wakeful nights, she fell asleep.

At this point one might well have asked Carrizales, if one hadn't known that he was asleep, what had happened to all his prudent precautions, his fears, his counsels, his judgements, the high walls of his house, his care lest even the shadow of one bearing a man's name should enter it, the close-kept revolving door, the thick walls, the blocked-up windows, the close confinement, the great dowry which he had given to Leonora, the continual gifts he gave her, the kind treatment of her maids and slave girls, the way in which he had taken care not to neglect any detail of all that he imagined they needed or could desire. But we have already said that there was no occasion for such a question, for he was sleeping a good deal more than was good for him. If he had heard and had perhaps answered, he would not have been able to give any better answer than to shrug his shoulders and raise his eyebrows and say, 'All this was brought to the ground by the cunning, as I see it, of an idle and vicious young man, and the malice of a false duenna, together with the ignorance of a girl who had been won over by persuasive appeals: God deliver us from enemies like this, against whom no shield of prudence nor sword of caution is effective.'

But all the same, Leonora's courage was such that the crucial moment showed her spirit in the face of the base attacks of her cunning assailant. They could not overcome her, so that he wore himself out in vain, she was victorious, and both fell asleep. And at this point heaven ordained that in spite of the ointment, Carrizales woke up, and as his custom was, felt the bed all over. Not finding his beloved wife in it, he leapt out of bed in fear and astonishment, with more speed and more spirit than might have been expected of one of his great age. When he failed to find his wife in the room, and saw that it was open and that the key was missing from its place between the mattresses, he thought he would go mad. But pulling himself together a little, he went out to the gallery and from there, a step at a time so that no one would hear him, he came to the room where the duenna was sleeping, and seeing her alone, without Leonora, he went to the duenna's room, and opening the door very gently he saw what he would prefer never to have seen, what he would have been glad not to have had eyes to see; he saw Leonora in Loaysa's arms, sleeping as soundly as if the ointment were working on them and not on him.

Carrizales's heart stopped beating when he saw this bitter sight; his voice stuck in his throat, his arms hung helplessly at his sides and he was like a cold marble statue; and although anger did what might have been expected, and stirred up his almost dying spirits, his grief was so strong that he could not breathe. Yet all the same he would have taken the vengeance which such a crime demanded if he had had the weapons wherewith to take it; so he resolved to return to his room to fetch a dagger, and to go back and remove the stains on his honour with the blood of his two enemies, and even with the blood of all his household. Having taken this honourable and necessary decision, he returned, as silently and cautiously as he had come, to his room, where grief and anguish so affected his heart that, unable to do anything else, he fell fainting on to his bed.

At last day came, and caught the adulterous couple entwined in each other's arms. Marialonso awoke, and was on the point of rushing off to claim what she thought was her due; but seeing that it was late, she decided to leave it for the following night. Leonora was alarmed when she saw that it was so late in the day, and cursed her carelessness and that of the wretched duenna. The two, full of alarm, went to the place where her husband was, praying silently to heaven that they would find him still snoring; and when they saw him lying quietly on his bed, they thought the ointment was still at work, for he was sleeping, and with great joy they embraced each other. Leonora went up to her husband, and grasping him by his arm she turned him from side to side, to see if he would wake up without their needing to wash him with vinegar, as they had been told was necessary for his recovery. But with the movement Carrizales recovered from his faint, and sighing deeply, in a feeble and sorrowful voice said,

'Woe is me, for to what a sad end my fortune has brought me!'

Leonora did not quite understand what her husband was saying, but seeing him awake and hearing him speak, she was surprised to see that the effect of the ointment had not lasted as long as they had told her, and went up to him. Putting her face close to his, and holding him in a close embrace, she said to him, 'What is the matter, my lord, for you seem to be in distress?'

The wretched old man heard the voice of his sweet enemy, and opening his eyes, in surprise and astonishment, he fixed them on her for a long time, at the end of which he said to her,

'Do me the favour, my lady, of sending straight away for your parents, because I feel a strange weariness in my heart and I am afraid I am soon going to die. I should like to see them before I go.'

Leonora was quite convinced that what her husband said was true, believing that the effect of the ointment, and not what he had seen, had reduced him to that state. She replied that she would do what he ordered, and sent the Negro to fetch her parents straight away. Then, embracing her husband, she caressed him more fondly than ever before, asking him how he felt, as tenderly and affectionately as if he were the person she loved best in the world. He looked at her in astonishment, as we have said, each word or caress being a sword-thrust that pierced his soul.

The duenna had told the household and Loaysa of her master's illness, impressing upon them that it must be serious, since he had forgotten to have the street doors closed when the Negro went out to fetch her mistress's parents. These folk were amazed at the summons too, because neither of them had set foot inside that house since their daughter had married. In short, they were all silent and baffled, not realizing the true cause of their master's illness. He would sigh every now and then so deeply and pitifully that his soul seemed to be torn from his body every time. Leonora wept when she saw him in that condition, and he laughed like one distracted at the thought of her false tears. At this point Leonora's parents arrived, and as they found the street door and the door into the patio open and the house silent and deserted, they were more than a little alarmed. They went to their son-in-law's room, and found him, as we've said, with his eyes still fixed on his wife, whom he held by the hand as they both wept, she at the mere sight of her husband's tears, he because he saw the deceit in hers.

As soon as her parents came in Carrizales began to speak, and this is what he said:

'Sit down, please, and all the rest of you leave the room, except for the lady Marialonso.'

They all did this, and when the five of them were alone, without waiting for anyone else to speak, Carrizales spoke calmly, wiping the tears from his eyes.

'I am quite sure, my parents and masters, that it will not be necessary to bring witnesses to make you believe the truth of what I want to tell you. You must well remember – for it is impossible that it should have slipped your memory – the love, the heart-felt emotion with which one year, one month, five days and nine hours ago you gave me your beloved daughter to be my lawful wife. You also know what a generous dowry I gave her, so lavish that it would have been enough to make more than three girls of her rank be considered rich. You must also recall the care I took to dress and adorn her with all that she desired and that I thought she ought to have. Furthermore you have seen, my lord and lady, how, as a result of my temperament, fearing that affliction from which I am doubtless going to die, and taught by the experience of my great age the many strange things that happen in this world, I tried to guard this jewel whom I chose and whom you gave me, with the greatest caution of which I was capable. I built up the walls of this house, I took the lights from the windows which looked on to the street, I doubled the locks on the doors, I put up a revolving door like a monastery, I banned from it for good and all everything which bore the sign or the name of a man, I gave her servants and slave girls to wait on her, I did not deny them or her anything they cared to ask of me, I made her my equal, I told her my most secret thoughts, I handed over my property to her. All these things were done, with due consideration, to ensure that I should enjoy without disturbance what had cost me such effort, and so that she should not give me any occasion for jealousy or fear of any kind; but as one cannot prevent by any human effort the punishment which the divine will chooses to inflict on those who do not centre all their desires and hopes in that will, it is no wonder that I should be disappointed in mine, and that I should myself have been the one to manufacture the poison which is killing me. But because I see that you are all puzzled as you hang on my words, I will bring to an end the long preamble to this speech of mine by telling you in one word what one could not properly say in a thousand. I declare then, ladies and gentlemen, that, after all I've said and done, this morning I found this girl, born into the world to destroy my peace and bring my life to an end' – and here he pointed to his wife – 'in the arms of a handsome young man, who is now shut up in the room of this obnoxious duenna.'

Carrizales had scarcely finished speaking when Leonora was struck with anguish and fell fainting at her husband's knees. Marialonso turned pale, and Leonora's parents were speechless. But going on Carrizales said,

'The vengeance which I wish to take for this injury neither is nor should be of the usual kind, for it is my wish that, just as I went to extremes in what I did, the vengeance I shall take should be of the same kind, inflicted upon myself by my own hand as the one who is most worthy of blame in this crime, for I should have considered that this girl's fifteen years would harmonize ill with the nearly eighty years of my life. I was like the silkworm, making the house in which I was to die. I do not blame you, ill-advised girl' – and saying this he bent and kissed the face of the fainting Leonora – 'I do not blame you, I say, because the persuasive tongues of crafty old women and the advances of enamoured youths easily conquer and triumph over the limited intelligence of those who are young. But so that all the world may see the extent of the good will and trust which I showed towards you, in these last moments of my life, I want to demonstrate it in a way that will be remembered in the world as an example if not of goodness, at least of unprecedented sincerity. So it is my wish that a notary be brought here immediately, so that I may make a new will, in which I shall have Leonora's dowry doubled, and shall beg her that after I am gone, which will be very soon, she make up her mind, which she will be able to do without effort, to marry that youth, whom the grey hairs of this dishonoured old man have never offended. In this way she will see that if in life I never for one moment departed from what I thought was her pleasure, in death I desire her to be happy with him whom she must love so much. The rest of my fortune I shall give to pious works; and to you, my lord and lady, I shall leave sufficient for you to live honourably for the rest of your lives. Let the notary come quickly, because my suffering is such that it will soon put an end to my life.'

When he had said this, he fell into a terrible faint, and dropped down so close to Leonora that their faces were together, a strange and sad sight for their parents, who saw their beloved daughter and their much loved son-in-law in this state. The evil duenna did not want to wait for the reproaches which she thought would be hurled at her by her lady's parents, so she rushed out of the room, and went to tell Loaysa of all that was going on, advising him to leave the house straight away, for she would take care to tell him through the Negro what happened, there being now neither doors nor keys to prevent it. Loaysa was amazed at what he heard, and taking her advice, he dressed up once more as a poor man and went to tell his friends of the strange, unprecedented turn his affairs had taken.

So while the couple were still unconscious, Leonora's father sent for a notary who was a friend of his, and who arrived by the time his daughter and son-in-law had recovered consciousness. Carrizales made a will in the terms he had mentioned, without declaring Leonora's guilt; and begging her moreover to marry, in the event of his death, the young man of whom he had privately spoken to her. When Leonora heard this, she threw herself at her husband's feet and, her heart beating furiously, said to him,

'May you live for many years, my dearest lord; for although you need not believe anything I may say, you should know that I have only offended you in thought.'

And beginning to make excuses and to tell the whole truth of the matter, she found she could not speak, and fainted again. The poor injured old man took her in his arms; her parents embraced her; and they all wept so bitterly that even the notary who was making the will was forced to weep too. In his will Carrizales left enough to keep all the servants in the house and let the slave girls and the Negro go free; and as for the false Marialonso, he simply ordered her to be paid her wages. A week later, overcome by grief, he was taken off to his grave.

Leonora was left to mourn him, a wealthy widow; and when Loaysa hoped to see fulfilled what he knew her husband had ordered in his will, he found instead that within a week she went off to be a nun in one of the most enclosed convents in the city. The young man went off in despair, and indeed in shame, to the Indies. Leonora's parents were desperately sad, although they found consolation in what their son-in-law had left them in his will. The servants were comforted too by what they inherited, and the slaves by their freedom; but the accursed duenna was left in poverty and disappointed of all her evil hopes.

And all I wanted was to get to the end of this affair, a memorable example which illustrates how little one should trust in keys, revolving doors and walls when the will remains free, and how much less one should trust youth and inexperience when confronted by the exhortation of these duennas in their black habits and their long, white head-dresses. The only thing that puzzles me is why Leonora did not make more effort to excuse herself and make her jealous husband realize how pure and innocent she was in that affair, but she was so confused that she was tongue-tied, and her husband died so soon that she could not find opportunity to explain herself.

Rinconete and Cortadillo

One hot summer day, two boys of about fourteen or fifteen turned up in the Molinillo inn, which is on the borders of the famous Alcudia plain, as you go from Castile to Andalusia. Certainly neither of them was more than seventeen, both of them were good-looking, but ragged, tattered and unkempt. They had no cloaks; their breeches were of drill and their stockings – of bare flesh. It's true that their footwear made up for it, because one of them wore rope sandals, but worn so much that they were in fact worn out, and the other had shoes which were full of holes and with the soles off, so that they were more like stocks than shoes. One of them wore a green hunting-cap; the other a hat without a band, low-crowned and broad-brimmed. In a bag on his back fastened round him one carried a greasy, chamois-coloured shirt; the other was empty-handed and with no baggage, although he had what looked like a big package inside his shirt-front, which turned out to be one of those so-called Walloon collars, stiffened with grease instead of starch, and so tattered that it seemed to be nothing but threads. Inside were some playing-cards of oval shape, for the corners had got worn out through use, and so that they would last a bit longer they had been clipped and left like that. The two were sunburnt, with long, dirty fingernails and hands none too clean; one had a cutlass, and the other a knife with a yellow horn handle, of the sort they call a cow-herd's knife.

The two of them came out to have their siesta on a sort of porch or shelter in front of the inn, and sat opposite each other.

The one who appeared to be the older said to the younger one, 'What part of the country do you come from, noble sir, and where are you going?'

'I don't know, sir Knight,' replied the other, 'where I came from, or where I am going either.'

'Well, certainly,' said the older one, 'you don't appear to come from heaven, and since this is no place to settle, you will certainly have to move on.'

'That is so,' replied the younger one, 'but I have spoken the truth in what I have said, because the place I came from is not my own part of the country. All I have in it is a father who doesn't treat me as his son and a stepmother who treats me in the way stepchildren are usually treated. I am going where chance directs, and I shall stop wherever I find someone who will give me the wherewithal to get through this wretched life.'

'And do you know any trade?' asked the big one.

The younger one replied, 'All I know is that I run like a hare, and jump like a deer and can cut very neatly with shears.'

'All that is very good, useful and profitable,' said the older one, 'because you'll always find a sacristan who'll give you the All Saints' offering to cut the paper flowers for the monument on Maundy Thursday.'

'That's not my kind of cutting,' answered the younger one. 'My father, by God's mercy, is a tailor and hosier, and he taught me how to cut the sort of leggings which cover the instep like spats, and I cut them so well that I could easily pass my master's examination, if my wretched luck didn't always do the dirty on me.'

'That happens to the best of us,' answered the big one, 'and I have always heard that the finest talents are the ones which most often go to waste, but you are still young enough to improve your fortune. And if I'm not mistaken and my eyes don't deceive me, you have other hidden gifts which you don't want to disclose.'

'Yes, I have,' answered the younger one, 'but they are not for publication, as you have clearly pointed out.'

To which the older one replied,

'Well, I can tell you that I am one of the best keepers of secrets you'll find for miles around, and to make you open your heart freely to me, I am going to put you under an obligation by opening mine first. I do this because I imagine that there's some good reason why fate has brought us together here, and I think we are destined to be true friends from now until our dying day. I, noble sir, am a native of Fuenfría, a place well known and famous by reason of the illustrious travellers who continually pass through it. My name is Pedro del Rincón; my father is a person of quality, being an officer of the Holy Crusade, by which I mean that he is a seller of papal bulls, or a pardoner as the common people call them. I went with him on his rounds once or twice, and I learnt his trade so well that the man who is reckoned to be the best seller of bulls in the world couldn't beat me at it. But one day, being more fond of the cash from the bulls than the bulls themselves, I made off with a bag of money and ended up with it in Madrid. Taking advantage of the sort of opportunities that crop up there, I very soon took the stuffing out of that bag and left it with more creases than a bridegroom's handkerchief. The man who had charge of the money came after me; they arrested me and I hadn't any influence; although, when these gentlemen saw how young I was, they were satisfied just to let them tie me to the doorknob and tickle my back for a bit, and banish me from the capital for four years. I was patient, shrugged my shoulders, put up with my punishment and my beating, and set off to do my exile, so speedily that I did not have a chance to find a mount. I took what I could of my valuables and the things that seemed most necessary to me, and among them I took these cards' – and with that he took out the ones which we've mentioned, which he had wrapped up in his collar – 'with which I've earned my keep in the inns and taverns all the way from Madrid to here, by playing pontoon. Although you can see that they're all dirty and worn, they can do wonders if you know them. You never cut without finding an ace underneath and, if you are versed in this game, you'll see what an asset it is to know that you have an ace for certain with the first card you take, which you can use as one or eleven: for the good thing is that when you get twenty-one, you keep the money. Apart from this, I learned from an ambassador's cook some tricks to use in playing reversis and lansquenet, which is also known as *andabobo*, for just as you might pass an examination in cutting leggings, so I could qualify as a master in the art of card-playing. This is enough to ensure that I shall not die of hunger, because even if I come to a farm, there's always someone who's ready to spend a bit of time playing cards. We two must try this experiment – let's cast the net and see if one of these muleteer-birds about here will fall into it. I mean we'll play pontoon as if we were in earnest, and if anyone wants to make a third, he'll be the first to lose his cash.'

'A splendid idea,' said the other, 'and I'm most grateful to you for having told me about your life, and so obliged me to tell you about mine. To cut a long story short this is it: I was born in a respectable village between Salamanca and Medina del Campo. My father is a tailor; he taught me his trade, and having started cutting with shears, my natural talent soon taught me to cut purses. The restricted life of the village and my stepmother's unloving attitude made me fed up, so I left my village and came to Toledo to practise my trade. I've done wonders at it, for there's not a locket hidden in a head-dress nor a pocket so well concealed that my fingers do not explore or my scissors cut it, even though the owners may be guarding it like Argus. And during the four months when I was in that city I was never once caught, attacked, chased by police, or split on by tale-bearers. It's true that about a week ago a double-crosser told the magistrate about my talents, and he, attracted by my gifts, wanted to see me; but I, being a humble person, and not wanting to have anything to do with such important people, contrived not to meet him, leaving the city so swiftly that I did not have time to fit myself out with a mount, money, hired coach, nor even a cart.'

'Forget it,' said Rincón, 'for now that we know each other, there's no occasion for these grand airs. Let's confess simply that we hadn't a bean, nor even any shoes.'

'All right,' answered Diego Cortado, for this is what the younger one said he was called, 'and since our friendship, as you, Mr Rinconete, have said, is destined to last for ever, let us initiate it with solemn and worthy ceremonies.'

And Diego Cortado, rising to his feet, embraced Rincón, and Rincón him, with equal affection. Then they both started to play pontoon with the aforementioned cards, free from dust and straw, but not from grease and cunning tricks; and after a few hands Cortado could turn up the ace as well as his teacher Rincón.

At this moment a muleteer came out to the porch to take the air, and asked if he could make a third. They welcomed him gladly, and in less than half an hour they won twelve *reales* and twenty-two *maravedís* from him, which was the same as giving him twelve stabs with a lance and twenty-two thousand sorrows. And the muleteer, thinking that because they were boys they would not be able to stop him, tried to take the money from them; but they, one with his cutlass and the other with his knife with the yellow handle, gave him so much to think about that if his companions hadn't come out he'd certainly have had a bad time.

At that moment a company of travellers on horseback happened to pass by on their way to take a rest at the Alcalde inn, which is half a league farther on. Seeing the muleteer quarrelling with the two boys, they managed to calm them down and invited them, if they were by any chance going to Seville, to accompany them.

'That's where we're going,' said Rincón, 'and we'll serve you in any way you may command.'

And without further delay, they jumped in front of the mules and went off with them, leaving the muleteer in a sorry plight and in a great rage, and the innkeeper's wife amazed at the behaviour of the two rogues; for she had been listening to their conversation without their knowing. When she told the muleteer that she had heard them say that the cards they had were faked, he tore his hair and wanted to go to the inn after them to recover his property, because he said it was a great insult and slight on his honour that two boys had deceived a full-grown man like him. His companions stopped him and advised him not to go, if only to avoid broadcasting his clumsiness and stupidity. In short, they argued with him to such effect that although they did not manage to console him they persuaded him to stay.

Meanwhile Cortado and Rincón contrived to serve the travellers so well that they carried them on their horses for most of the way, and although they had some chances to rob the bags of their temporary masters, they didn't take them, so as not to lose the splendid chance of the journey to Seville, where they very much wanted to go. All the same, as they were going through the Aduana gate into the city at prayer time, Cortado, taking advantage of the inspection and the payment of duty, could not refrain from cutting the bag or valise that a certain Frenchman in the company was carrying on the crupper of his mule. So, with his yellow-handled knife he gave it such a long and deep wound that its insides were open for all to see, and he neatly took from it two good shirts, a sundial and a little memo book, things which they didn't much like the look of. They thought that if the Frenchman was carrying that valise on the crupper of his horse, it was a pity to have filled it with things of such little consequence as these trinkets, and they would have liked to give it another touch; but they didn't, thinking that it would already have been missed and the rest put in a safe place.

They had taken their leave of the party who had supported them so far on their journey before performing this robbery, and the next day they sold the shirts in the second-hand shop near the Arenal gate, and made twenty *reales* out of them. After this they went to look at the city, and were amazed at the size and splendour of its cathedral and the vast number of people by the river, because it was at the time when they were loading up the fleet. There were six galleys there, the sight of which made them sigh and dread the day when a mistake on their part would lead them to spend the rest of their lives in them. They saw the vast number of basket-boys who were running about there, and they inquired of one of them what sort of business they were engaged in, if it was hard work, and what they made out of it. An Asturian boy, who was the one they questioned, said that it was an easy trade and that you didn't pay any duty, and that some days he made five or six *reales* profit. With that he could eat, drink and live splendidly, without needing to look for a master to whom he would have to give guarantees; and knowing that he could eat at any time he wished, for he could find food at all times of the day in any cheap eating-house in the city.

The account given by the little Asturian didn't seem at all bad to them, and the trade seemed just made for them, for they could practise their own safely under cover of it, through the opportunity it offered of going into all the houses. They decided there and then to buy the necessary equipment to practise it, since they could engage in it without passing any examination. And the Asturian, in answer to their question about what they should buy, told them they would each need a small bag, clean if not new, and three palm baskets each, two big and one small, in which the meat, fish and fruit could be put, the bag being for the bread; and he took them to where they could sell it. They, with the money left from the loot from the Frenchman, bought the whole outfit, and in two hours, they were past masters at the new trade, such skill did they show in displaying their baskets and arranging their bags. Their guide showed them the places where they should go: in the mornings, to the meat market and San Salvador Square; on fish days to the fish market and the Costanilla; every afternoon to the river; on Thursdays to the Feria.

They made a note of all this, and the next morning very early they stationed themselves in San Salvador Square. They had barely arrived when they were surrounded by other boys engaged in the same trade, who seeing their brand-new bags and baskets realized that they were new to the square. They asked them thousands of questions, and they answered all of them sensibly and politely. Then a student and a soldier came up, and attracted by the cleanness of the baskets of the two novices, the one who appeared to be a student called Cortado, while the soldier called Rincón:

'God be with you,' they said in unison.

'That's a good start to our business,' said Rincón, 'for you're the first to employ me, sir.'

To which the soldier replied, 'It's not a bad beginning, because I'm in funds and I'm in love, and I'm giving a dinner-party today for some friends of my lady-love.'

'Then load me up as much as you like, sir, for I've got the will and the strength to carry the whole square, and if you need my help to cook it, I'll do it very willingly.'

The soldier was very pleased with the boy's good humour, and told him that if he wanted to go into service, he would rescue him from that wretched trade; to which Rincón replied that as that was the first day he had practised it, he didn't want to leave it so soon, until he had at least weighed up the pros and cons. If he didn't like it, he gave him his word that he would rather serve him than a canon.

The soldier laughed, loaded him up well, showed him his lady's house so that he should know it from then on and so that he would have no need to go with the boy when he sent him again. Rincón promised to be loyal and treat him fairly; the soldier gave him three pennies and he rushed back to the square, so as not to lose the chance of another job. The Asturian had told him about this trick; and also that when they were carrying small fish, such as dace or sardines or plaice, they could take a few out by way of samples, at least against the day's expenses; but that this had to be done with care, so that one should not lose one's good reputation, which was what counted most in that trade.

Quick as Rincón was in getting back, he found Cortado already installed in the same spot. Cortado went up to Rincón, and asked him how things had gone with him. Rincón opened his hand and showed him the three pennies. Cortado put his hand into his shirt-front and took out a small purse, which gave signs of having been scented with amber in times gone by. It was rather bulky, and he said, 'This is what his reverence the student paid me with, and he gave me two pennies as well; but you take it, Rincón, in case anything happens.'

When the purse had already been handed over unobserved, the student suddenly arrived, sweating profusely and in a terrible state. Seeing Cortado he asked him if by chance he had seen a purse of such and such a kind, which he had lost, with fifteen real golden crowns and three *reales* and the same number of *maravedís* in pennies and halfpence, and whether he had taken it while he was going round with him doing his shopping. To which Cortado, dissembling with remarkable skill, and without showing any sign of being disturbed or changing his expression, replied, 'All I can say about this purse is that you must have been very careless to have lost it.'

'That's just it, wretch that I am!' answered the student. 'I must have been very careless with it, for it's been stolen from me.'

'That's what I say,' said Cortado, 'but while there's life there's hope, and your best hope is to be patient, for God made us out of nothing, one day follows another, and what they give they take away; and perhaps as time goes on, the one who took the purse may come to repent and return it to you smelling of incense.'

'We could manage without the incense,' answered the student.

And Cortado went on to say, 'Especially as there are papal letters of excommunication and there is diligence, which is the mother of good fortune. All the same, I shouldn't like to be the one who took that purse, because if you are in holy orders of any kind, I'd think I had committed some great incest or sacrilege.'

'He certainly has committed sacrilege,' said the disconsolate student; 'for although I'm not a priest, I am sacristan to some nuns, and the money in the purse was from the stipend of a chaplaincy, which a friend of mine who is a priest asked me to collect, and it is sacred and holy money.'

'That's his funeral,' said Rincón at this point. 'He asked for it. There's a day of judgement, when everything will come to light, and then we'll see whom we're dealing with, and who was the bold fellow who dared to take, steal and appropriate the stipend of the chaplaincy. And how much does he make a year? Tell me, Sacristan, for goodness' sake.'

'Make, be damned. Am I going to waste my time telling you about how much he makes?' answered the sacristan, bursting with anger. 'Tell me, brother, if you know anything; if not, God be with you, for I'm going to make a public declaration of the theft.'

'That doesn't seem a bad solution,' said Cortado, 'but be sure you don't forget what the purse looks like, nor the exact amount of money in it; for if you're a farthing out, it will never appear as long as the world lasts, and that's as true as fate.'

'There's no fear of that,' answered the sacristan, 'for it's more fixed in my memory than the peal of the bells: I shan't be a mite out.'

At this point he took out of his pocket a lace-edged handkerchief to wipe the sweat off his brow, for it was pouring off him, and as soon as Cortado saw it, he marked it down as his. So when the sacristan had gone, Cortado followed him, and caught him up at the Gradas, where he called him and drew him aside. Then he began to say such nonsense to him and tell him such tall stories about the theft and discovery of his purse, raising his hopes, without ever finishing any of the arguments he started, that the poor sacristan was quite bewildered as he listened to him; and as he couldn't manage to understand what he was saying to him, he made him repeat the argument two or three times. Cortado looked him straight in the face and didn't take his eyes off his; the sacristan was staring back at him, hanging on his words. This tremendous fascination gave Cortado a chance to finish off the job, and he neatly extracted the handkerchief from his pocket. Then, saying goodbye to him, he told him to try to see him in the same place in the afternoon, because he had an idea that a boy who followed the same trade and was about the same size as he, and who had thieving tendencies, had taken the purse, and that he undertook to find out, sooner or later.

The sacristan was somewhat consoled when he heard this, and left him. Cortado came up to Rincón, who had seen it all from a little way off; and farther on there was another basket-boy, who saw all that had happened and how Cortado gave the handkerchief to Rincón. Going up to them he said,

'Tell me, gallant sirs, do you belong to the bad set or not?'

'We don't understand what you are on about, gallant sir,' answered Rincón.

'You don't understand when I say thieves?'

'We're not from Thebes nor from Murcia,' said Cortado. 'If you want anything else, say so; if not, be off with you.'

'Don't you understand?' said the youth. 'Well I'll make you understand, and I'll feed it to you with a silver spoon. I mean, gentlemen, are you thieves? But I don't know why I'm asking you this, for I already know you are. Tell me, how is it you haven't been to Mr Monipodio's customs-house?'

'Do you pay duty on thefts in this part of the country, gallant sir?' said Rincón.

'If you don't pay,' answered the boy, 'at least you register with Mr Monipodio, who is the father, master and protector of thieves; and so I advise you to come with me and pay your respects to him, or if not, don't dare to steal without his authority, or it'll cost you dear.'

'I thought,' said Cortado, 'that stealing was a free trade, exempt from tax or tribute, and that if you do pay it, you pay wholesale, giving your neck and your back by way of settlement. But since things are this way, and every country has its customs, let us observe those of this country, which since it is the most important in the world will be the most proper as regards its customs. So you may conduct us to the place where this gentleman you mention is to be found, for I already have an idea, from what I've heard, that he is very well qualified and noble, and extremely skilled at his trade.'

'Indeed he is able, skilled and well qualified,' answered the youth. 'So much so, that during the four years that he's been our chief and our father not more than four of us have ended up on the gallows, only about thirty have had tannings and sixty-two gone to the galleys.'

'Indeed, sir,' said Rincón, 'I can no more understand what you are saying than fly.'

'Let's be on our way, for I'll explain as we go,' answered the young man; 'as well as other things which you ought to know like the back of your hand.'

And so as they walked on he explained to them other words belonging to what they call 'gipsy language' or 'thieves' slang', in the course of his talk, which was by no means short, for the road was long. On the way Rincón said to his guide, 'Are you by any chance a thief?'

'Yes,' he replied, 'in the service of God and all good folk, although not a very expert one, for I'm still in my novice year.'

To which Cortado replied, 'It's news to me that there are thieves in the world in the service of God and good folk.'

To which the boy replied, 'Sir, I don't get mixed up in things I don't understand; what I know is that each one in his profession can praise God, and especially when things are so well ordered as they are under Monipodio.'

'Without doubt,' said Rincón, 'it must be a good and holy order since it makes thieves serve God.'

'It is so holy and so good,' replied the boy, 'that I don't know if it would be possible to improve on it in our craft. He has laid it down that out of what we steal we give something by way of alms to pay for oil for the lamp which burns in front of a most sacred image in this city, and indeed we have seen great things as a result of this good work. Some days ago they inflicted the *ansia* three times on a *cuatrero* who had stolen a couple of *roznos*, and although he was thin and sickly, he endured it without squealing, as if it were nothing. We in the profession attribute this to his piety, for he's not really strong enough to suffer the *primer desconcierto* of the torturer's rope. And because I know you are going to ask me about some of the words I've been using, prevention is better than cure, so I'll tell you before you ask me. You must know that a *cuatrero* is a horse-thief; *ansia* is a torture; *roznos* are asses, speaking with respect; *primer desconcierto* is the first twist of the rope. Other things we do, like saying our rosary once a week, and many of us don't steal on a Friday, nor do we speak to a woman called Mary on a Saturday.'

'All this seems delightful to me,' said Cortado, 'but tell me, is any other restitution or penance demanded apart from what you've said?'

'There's no question of restitution,' answered the boy. 'That is impossible; for the stolen goods are divided up, and each one of the members and contracting parties takes his share. So the one who first did the stealing cannot give anything back, especially since there is no one to make us do it, for we never go to confession. And if they excommunicate us, the news never reaches us, because we never go to church at the time when the decrees are read, except on feast days, for the sake of the profit which the crowds provide.'

'And do these gentlemen say,' asked Cortado, 'that their life is holy and good just because they do things like that?'

'Well, what's wrong with it?' replied the boy. 'Isn't it worse to be a heretic or a renegade, or to kill one's father and mother, or to be a solomite?'

'You must mean "sodomite",' said Rincón.

'That's what I say,' said the boy.

'It's all just as bad,' Cortado went on. 'But since our fate has decreed that we should join this brotherhood, let's get moving, for I'm dying to meet Mr Monipodio, of whose many virtues I hear so much.'

'Your wish will soon be fulfilled,' said the boy, 'for you can see his house from here. Stay at the door, and I'll go in and see if he's free, because this is the time when he usually sees people.'

'All right,' said Rincón.

And going on a little, the boy went into a house, which didn't look very impressive – in fact it looked exactly the opposite –

and the two of them waited at the door. He soon came out and called them, and they went in. Their guide told them to wait in a little courtyard paved with brick, which was so spotlessly clean that it shone as if it had been rubbed with the finest vermilion. On one side was a three-legged stool and on the other a pitcher with a broken lip, with a little jug on top, suffering from the same complaint as the pitcher; on the other side was a rush mat, and in the middle a pot, which they call a *maceta* in Seville, with sweet basil in it.

The boys examined the furnishings in the house with care until Mr Monipodio came down; and seeing that he was a long time, Rincón ventured into one of the two small rooms which led off the courtyard. In it were two fencing swords and two cork shields, hanging from four nails, and a big chest, without a lid or any kind of cover, and three more rush mats spread out on the floor. There was one of those badly-printed images of Our Lady stuck on the wall opposite, lower down a little palm basket and, fixed to the wall, a white bowl, from which Rincón concluded that the basket served as an alms box, and the bowl to hold holy water, as was in fact the case.

At this point, two youths of about twenty and dressed as students came into the house and, shortly afterwards, two basket-boys and a blind man. Without saying a word, they began to walk up and down in the courtyard. Soon after, two old men dressed in thick flannel came in, each wearing spectacles, which made them look venerable and respectable, and each with a rosary of jingling beads in his hand. After them entered an old woman with a long full skirt, and, without saying a word, she went into the room and, having taken holy water, knelt down very devoutly in front of the image. After some time, she kissed the ground and raised her arms and eyes to heaven three times.

Then she got up, threw her offering into the basket, and went out with the rest into the patio. Within a short time there were about fourteen persons assembled in the patio in different dress and belonging to different professions. Among the last to arrive were two fine swaggering young fellows, with big moustaches, broad-brimmed hats, Walloon collars, coloured stockings, fancy garters, outsize swords, a pocket pistol each instead of a dagger, and with their bucklers hanging from their belts. As soon as they came in, these two cast suspicious glances at Rincón and Cortado, as if surprised to see them and not knowing who they were. And going up to them, they asked them if they belonged to the brotherhood. Rincón answered 'yes', and that they were at their service.

At last the moment arrived when Mr Monipodio came down, all the more welcome for having been awaited so long by that virtuous company. He looked about forty-five or forty-six years old, tall, dark, beetle-browed, and with a very thick black beard and deep-set eyes. He was in his shirt-sleeves, and through the opening in front you could see a veritable wood, so thick was the hair on his chest. He wore a thick flannel cloak reaching almost to his feet, on which he wore a pair of shoes which he had left unfastened. His legs were covered by ill-fitting drill breeches, which were baggy and reached to his ankles. His hat was one of those worn by the gentry of the underworld, with a broad brim and a crown shaped like a bell, and he wore a shoulder-belt, from which hung a short sword with the 'little dog' mark. His hands were short and hairy, and his fingers fat, with fingernails splayed out and bent under. His legs were not visible, but his feet were enormously broad with bunions on them. In fact, he looked the most clumsy and hideous ruffian you've ever seen. The boys' guide came in with him and, seizing them by the hands, presented them to Monipodio, saying to him, 'These are the two good lads I told you about, Mr Monipodio. 'Samine them, and you'll see how worthy they are to enter our fraternity.'

'I'll be very glad to do that,' answered Monipodio.

I forgot to say that as soon as Monipodio came downstairs, all those who were waiting for him bowed long and low to him, except the two toughs, who in a cool sort of way, as they put it themselves, took off their hats to him, and then went back to walking up and down one side of the courtyard, while Monipodio walked up and down the other, asking the newcomers about their trade, where they came from and who their parents were.

To which Rincón replied, 'The trade speaks for itself, since we have come to you; where we come from doesn't seem to matter much, nor who our parents are, because you don't have to provide this sort of information even to enter an order of nobility.'

To which Monipodio replied, 'You are right, my son, and it is a very proper thing to conceal these things, as you say; for if fortune doesn't turn out as it should, it is not a good thing that there should be an entry in the register with the notary's signature over it, with the words, "So-and-so, son of so-and-so, native of such-and-such a place, was hanged, or whipped on such-and-such a day," or something of that kind, for it sounds bad to sensitive ears. And so I repeat that it is a good idea to keep quiet about where you come from, to conceal your parentage, and to change your own name, although in our company nothing must be concealed. For the moment all I want to know is your names.'

Rincón told his, and Cortado too.

'Well, from now on,' said Monipodio, 'I wish and indeed insist that you, Rincón, shall be called "Rinconete", and you,

Cortado, "Cortadillo", which are names just right for your age and our rules, which require us to know the names of the parents of our fellow-members. This is because it is our custom every year to have certain Masses said for the souls of those who are deceased and for our benefactors, paying the priest's stipend with part of our takings, and these Masses, once said and paid for, they say are profitable to the said souls by way of outrage. Under the heading of our benefactors we include the attorney who defends us, the bailiff who warns us, the executioner who has pity on us, the man who, when one of us is running away down the street and someone shouts after him, "Stop thief! Stop thief!", stands in the way and holds up the stream of people following him, saying, "Let the poor wretch go, he's been unlucky enough already! Let him get away; let his sin be his punishment!" The girls who take pains to help us both in prison and in the galleys are our benefactors too; and so are our fathers and mothers, who cast us into the world, and the notary, who if he is in a good mood plays down our crimes and gets us off lightly. For all of these that I've mentioned our brotherhood holds its adversary every year with the greatest pump and salinity we can manage.'

'Certainly,' said Rinconete, who had already adopted his new name, 'it is a task worthy of that most lofty and profound talent which, so we have heard, you, Mr Monipodio, possess. But our parents are still alive; if in their lifetime we should come across them, we shall immediately inform this most happy and friendly confraternity, so that they may benefit from this outrage or torment, or that adversary you mention, with the accustomed solemnity and pomp, if it wouldn't be more properly done with "pump" and "salinity", as you also noted in your statement.'

'It shall be done, or strike me dead,' replied Monipodio.

And calling the guide, he said to him, 'Come here, Ganchuelo. Are the guards posted?'

'Yes,' said the guide, whose name was Ganchuelo. 'There are three guards keeping watch, and there's no fear of our being caught unawares.'

'Returning, then, to our business,' said Monipodio, 'I should like you to tell me, boys, what you know, so as to give you the duty appropriate to your inclination and talent.'

'I,' answered Rinconete, 'know a bit about card tricks. I can keep a card back; I can recognize marked cards; I can play with one, or four, or eight; I'm not slow when it comes to marking cards so that you can recognize them by touch; I can make a gap in a pack as easily as I can get into my house, I'd sooner get together a band of sharpers than a regiment in Naples, and I'd slip a bad card to a chap faster than I'd lend him two *reales*.'

'That's a start,' said Monipodio, 'but all that is old stuff, and so well worn that every novice knows all about it, so it's no use except with people so green that they let themselves be killed before midnight. But time will tell, and we shall see what we shall see; for half a dozen lessons on top of this foundation I should think would make you a first-rate operator, and even a master of the craft.'

'All that will be in the service of your worship and the members of the brotherhood,' answered Rinconete.

'And you, Cortadillo, what do you know?' asked Monipodio.

'I,' answered Cortadillo, 'know the trick called put in two and take out five, and I can explore a pocket with great accuracy and skill.'

'Do you know anything more?' said Monipodio.

'No, for my great sins,' answered Cortadillo.

'Don't be upset, my son,' replied Monipodio, 'for you have

come to a refuge where you will not founder and a school from which you are bound to emerge with great profit in all those things that most concern you. And when it comes to spirit, how are you off, boys?'

'How do you think?' answered Rinconete. 'We've enough spirit to undertake anything to do with our craft and profession.'

'Good,' replied Monipodio; 'but I should like you also to be able, if necessary, to stand half a dozen *ansias* without opening your mouth, or saying a word.'

'We know already,' said Cortadillo, 'what *ansias* means, and we're ready for anything. We're not so ignorant that we haven't grasped that what the tongue says the neck pays for, and heaven is kind to the man of courage, if we may use the term, when it leaves it to his tongue to determine whether he lives or dies. For after all, there's only a letter's difference between a "yes" and a "no".'

'Stop, that's enough,' said Monipodio at this point. 'This statement alone convinces me, and obliges me to let you become full members at once and dispense with the year of probation.'

'I agree to that,' said one of the toughs.

And with one voice all the company agreed, for they had been listening to the whole conversation, and they begged Monipodio to allow them straight away to enjoy the immunities of the brotherhood, because their pleasant bearing and good conversation well deserved this reward. He answered that, to please them all, he would grant this immediately, bidding them realize the importance of these immunities, since they involved not having to pay half the proceeds of the first theft they made, nor to do menial jobs all that year, such as taking bail to the prison for a senior member or going to the brothel on behalf of those who had contributed. They could drink wine without water in it, have a party whenever, however and wherever they wished, without asking leave of their chief; have a share straight away in the winnings of the senior members of the brotherhood; and other things which they considered to be a great privilege, and for which they thanked the company in the most civil manner.

At this point, a boy came running in out of breath, and said,

'The constable in charge of vagrants is coming towards the house, but he has no patrol with him.'

'Don't get excited,' said Monipodio, 'for he's a friend and never comes to do us any harm. Be calm, and I'll go out and talk to him.'

They were all rather frightened, but they calmed down, and Monipodio went out to the door, where he found the constable, to whom he stayed talking for a while. When he came back in again, he asked,

'Who was on today in San Salvador Square?'

'I was,' said the guide.

'Well, how is it,' said Monipodio, 'that I haven't been shown a little amber purse which went astray there this morning, with fifteen gold crowns and two *reales* and I don't know how many pennies?'

'It's true,' said the guide, 'that that purse was missing today; but I haven't taken it, nor can I imagine who did.'

'None of your tricks with me,' said Monipodio. 'The purse must be produced because the constable is asking for it, and he's a friend and does us thousands of favours every year!'

The boy swore again that he knew nothing about it. Monipodio began to get so angry that it looked as if he was shooting fire from his eyes, as he said, 'Let no one make light of breaking our rule in the slightest degree, or it'll cost him his life! Out with the purse, and if it's being concealed so as not to pay the dues, I will pay the lot on my own account, because the constable must be satisfied whatever happens.'

The youth swore and cursed again, saying that he hadn't taken the purse nor set eyes on it; all of which added fuel to the flames of Monipodio's anger, and made the whole gathering get excited, seeing that their statutes and good ordinances were being broken.

Rinconete, seeing all this dissension and excitement, thought it a good idea to calm it down, and to satisfy his chief, who was bursting with rage. So, taking counsel with his friend Cortadillo, with his consent he took out the sacristan's purse and said, 'Let's put an end to this quarrel, gentlemen, for this is the purse, and nothing is missing of what the constable has mentioned. My comrade, Cortadillo, took it, with a handkerchief belonging to the same owner, for good measure.'

Then Cortadillo took out the handkerchief and showed it to the company. When Monipodio saw this, he said, 'Cortadillo the good (for you must answer to this name and title from now on), you must keep the handkerchief, and I undertake to pay compensation for this. As for the purse, the constable must have it, for it belongs to a sacristan who is a relative of his, and it is only right that the proverb should be proved right which says: "The least you can do is give a leg of the chicken to the man who gave you the whole bird." This good constable covers up more in one day than we can or do give him in a hundred.'

By common consent, they all applauded the splendid behaviour of the two newcomers and the judgement and decision of their leader, who went out to give the purse to the constable. Cortadillo was confirmed in his surname of 'Good', just as if he were Don Alonso Pérez de Guzmán the Good – the one who threw the knife over the walls of Tarifa to cut off the head of his only son.

When Monipodio came back, two girls came in with him, with painted faces, reddened lips and their bosoms covered with white lead. They wore short camlet cloaks, and were a brazen-looking couple of hussies. As soon as they saw them Rinconete and Cortadillo recognized that they were from the bawdy-house, and they were quite right. As soon as they came in, they went with open arms towards Chiquiznaque and Maniferro, the two toughs (the name Maniferro was because he had an iron hand in place of one which had been cut off by order of the Court). They embraced the girls with great delight, and asked them if they had brought anything to wet their whistle.

'Well, what do you think, my brave lad?' answered one of them, who was called Gananciosa. 'Your boy Silbatillo will soon be home with the laundry basket stuffed with what God has been pleased to provide.'

And so it was, for immediately in came a boy with a laundry basket covered with a sheet.

They were all delighted to see Silbatillo come in, and immediately Monipodio ordered them to get out one of the rush mats which were in the room and to spread it out in the middle of the courtyard. And then he ordered everyone to sit down in a circle; because once they'd had a bite, they would get down to business. Then the old woman who had prayed to the image said,

'Monipodio, my boy, I'm not in a mood for parties, for I have had a dizzy head for two days and it's driving me mad. Anyway before midday I must go and carry out my devotions and place my candles before the altars of Our Lady of the Waters and the Holy Crucifix of St Augustine, which I'd have to do even if it snowed or blew a gale. What I've come for is to tell you that last night Renegado and Centopiés brought a laundry basket to my house, a bit bigger than this one, full of washing, and I declare with the soap still on it and all. The poor things couldn't have had time to get rid of it, and they were sweating so much that it was a shame to see them come staggering in with the water streaming down their faces, like little angels. They told me they were going after a shepherd who had been weighing some sheep in the Carnicería to see if they couldn't get a touch from a magnificent bag of *reales* he was carrying. They didn't unpack or count the clothes, trusting my honesty; and as I hope that God will grant my good wishes and free us all from the power of the law I haven't touched the basket, and it's as sound as the day it was made.'

'We'll believe all you say, mother,' answered Monipodio, 'and let the basket stay there, for I'll go at nightfall, and examine what's in it, and give each one his due, as truly and faithfully as I always do.'

'As you decide, son,' answered the old woman; 'and as it's getting late, give me a swig if you have one to comfort this poor old stomach of mine. It's in such a poor state.'

'You shall have it, mother,' said Escalanta, Gananciosa's companion.

And when the basket was uncovered, there was a kind of leather bag with about eight gallons of wine and a cork measure which could take about a couple of litres easily; and when Escalanta had filled it, she put it in the hands of the devout old woman, who taking it with both hands, and blowing off some foam, said: 'You've poured a lot out, daughter Escalanta; but God will give me strength for all my tasks.'

And putting it to her lips, without taking breath, she

transferred it from the measure to her stomach in one go, and said as she finished,

'It's from Guadalcanal, and the little chap still has a tiny trace of chalk in him. God comfort you, daughter, as you have comforted me; although I'm afraid it won't do me much good, for I had no breakfast.'

'It certainly won't, mother,' answered Monipodio, 'because it's extremely old.'

'By the Virgin I hope it is,' answered the old woman.

And she added, 'Girls, see if you have a penny to buy the candles for my prayers, because in my haste and eagerness to bring you the news about the basket I left my bag at home.'

'Yes, I have one, Señora Pipota' (for that was the name of the good old woman), answered Gananciosa. 'Here you are. I'll give you two pennies, and I beg you to buy a candle for me with one of them, and put it in front of St Michael; and if you can buy two, put the other one in front of St Blas, for they are my patrons. I should like you to put another in front of Santa Lucia, because I'm devoted to her too, for my eyes' sake, but I haven't any change. Never mind; we'll have enough to deal with them all another day.'

'Just you do that, daughter, and mind you're not mean; for it's very important to do your good deeds before you die, and not to wait until your heirs or executors do them.'

'Mother Pipota is right,' said Escalanta. And putting her hand in her purse, she gave her another penny, and asked her to put another couple of candles in front of the saints who in her opinion were most profitable and appreciative.

With that, Pipota said to them as she went off, 'Enjoy yourselves, children, while you have time; for old age will come, and then you will mourn the times you wasted in your youth, as I

70

mourn them; and commend me to God in your prayers, for I am going to do the same for myself and for you, so that He may keep us free and safe, in our dangerous business, from the terror of the law.'

And with that, she left them.

When the old woman had gone, they all sat round the mat and Gananciosa spread out the sheet to serve as a tablecloth. The first thing she took out of the basket was a great bunch of radishes and about two dozen oranges and lemons, and then a big pan full of slices of fried cod; then she put out half a Dutch cheese, a pot of excellent olives, and a plate of prawns, a great dish of crabs, with a caper and pimento sauce, and three snowy white loaves from Gandul. There were about fourteen for lunch, and every one of them took out a knife with a yellow handle, except for Rinconete, who took out his cutlass. The two old men in flannel cloaks and the guide had the job of pouring out the wine from the cork measure. But they had barely begun to attack the oranges, when they were all startled by a knocking at the door. Monipodio told them to be calm, and going into the lower room, he took a buckler off a hook and went to the door with his hand on his sword, and in a deep and frightening voice asked, 'Who's there?'

The reply came from outside, 'It's nobody of consequence, Mr Monipodio; only Tagarete, on guard duty this morning; and I've come to say that Juliana La Cariharta is coming this way, all dishevelled and in tears, and she looks as if something terrible's happened to her.'

At that moment, the person mentioned arrived, sobbing, and when Monipodio recognized her, he opened the door, and told Tagarete to go back to his post and henceforth report what he saw with less noise and fuss; which he said he would.

Cariharta came in, a girl got up like the others and belonging to the same profession. Her hair was dishevelled and her face was all bruised, and as soon as she got into the courtyard she fell fainting on the ground. Gananciosa and Escalanta rushed to help her and, unfastening her blouse, found her all blackened and battered. They threw water in her face, and she recovered, and shouted out,

'Let the justice of God and the King fall on that shameless ruffian, on that cowardly thief, on that lousy rogue whom I've saved from the gallows more times than he has hairs in his beard! Woe is me! To think I've wasted my youth and the best years of my life for a soulless, wicked, incorrigible wretch like that!'

'Calm down, Cariharta,' said Monipodio at this point; 'for I'm here and I'll see that justice is done. Tell us what they've done to you, for it'll take longer for you to tell us about it than for me to see you revenged; let me know if you've had any trouble with your boy friend, for if this is the case and you want vengeance, you need only say the word.'

'Boy friend?' replied Juliana, 'I'd sooner have a boy friend in hell than that lion among lambs and that lamb among men. Do you think I'd ever eat or go to bed with that one again? I'd rather be eaten by jackals, after he's left me in the state I'm in now.'

And lifting her skirts up to her knees, and even a little higher, she showed that they were covered with weals.

'This is how that wretched Repolido has left me,' she went on, 'when he owes me more than the mother who bore him. And why do you think he did it? As if I gave him any occasion for it. Not on your life. All he did it for was because as he was gambling and started to lose, he sent me his boy Cabrillas to ask me for thirty *reales*, and I sent him only twenty-four, and

72

may God grant that the labour and anxiety I had to get them may be set against my sins. And in payment for this kindness and good deed, thinking that I was keeping something back from the amount he imagined I had, this morning he dragged me out behind the Huerta del Rey, and there, among some olive trees, he stripped me and with his belt, without bothering to hold the buckle (curse him and may I see him in fetters), he whipped me so many times that he left me for dead; and these weals that you can see will testify to the truth of my story.'

Then she began to shout again, and to demand justice; and Monipodio and all the toughs who were there promised again to satisfy her.

Gananciosa took her hand to comfort her, telling her that she would very willingly give one of the best jewels she possessed to have had the same thing happen to her with her boy friend.

'Because I want you to know, Sister Cariharta, if you don't know already, that to be beaten is a sign of affection; and when these rogues attack and beat and kick us, then they adore us. If this is not true, tell me this: after Repolido had punished you, and beaten you up, didn't he pet you a bit?'

'A bit?' she replied in tears. 'A hundred thousand times, and he'd have given his right hand to have me go back to his lodgings with him; and in fact I think he nearly wept himself after he had beaten me.'

'I don't doubt it,' replied Gananciosa; 'and he would weep now if he saw the state he'd left you in; for these men, in cases like this, have barely committed the sin when they are overcome by remorse. You'll see, sister, that he'll come and look for you before we leave here, and ask your forgiveness for all that has happened, as quiet as a lamb.'

'Indeed,' said Monipodio, 'the wretched coward will not

darken these doors if he doesn't first do public penance for the crime he's committed. How dare he put his hands on Cariharta's face, or her flesh, a girl who's as clean and hard-working as Gananciosa herself, and I can't praise her more highly than that.'

'Oh, Mr Monipodio,' said Juliana, 'don't say anything against the wretch; for bad as he is I love him more than my own life, and the arguments that my friend Gananciosa has put forward in his favour have convinced me. In fact I'm inclined to go and look for him.'

'You won't if you take my advice,' replied Gananciosa, 'because he'll get all puffed up and be up to all sorts of tricks with you. Keep calm, sister, for you'll soon have him coming to say he's sorry, just as I've said; and if he doesn't come we'll write him some verses that will show him where he gets off.'

'Yes, indeed,' said Cariharta, 'for I've plenty of things to write to him!'

'I shall act as secretary when required,' said Monipodio, 'and although I'm no poet, if a man makes up his mind, he'll write a couple of thousand verses in next to no time; and if they don't come out as they should, I have a friend who's a barber and a great poet, who'll fill up the verses any time you like. But for the moment let's finish our lunch, for all the rest can wait till afterwards.'

Juliana was happy to obey her chief, so they all went back to their merry-making, and soon saw the bottom of the basket and the dregs of the wineskin. The old men drank without stopping; the young ones freely; the ladies without stinting themselves. The old men then asked to be excused, and Monipodio gave permission immediately; telling them to come straight away and tell him anything that might be useful and profitable to the community. They replied that they would take good care to do so, and went off. Rinconete, who was curious by nature, having first begged leave, asked Monipodio what the use was to the community of this pair, who were so old, so broken down and seedy. To which Monipodio replied that these, according to their jargon and way of speaking, were called 'hornets', and that their job was to go round by day to see which houses they could break into by night, and to follow those who got money out of the Contratación, or Mint, to see where they went with it and even where they deposited it. When they found out they tested the thickness of the wall of the house concerned and marked the most suitable place to make the holes to enable them to get in. In short, he said that they were quite as valuable as anyone in the fraternity, if not more so, and that they kept a fifth of everything that was stolen through their efforts, like the King with treasure-trove; and that for all that, they were honourable and truthful men, who led a good life, and had a good reputation, feared God and their consciences, and heard Mass most devoutly every day.

'And there are some of them who are so frugal, especially these two who've just gone off, that they are content with much less than is their due according to our tariff. There are another two who are public porters, who, as they are always moving house, know how to get in and out of all the houses in the city, and which houses are worth while and which are not.'

'All this seems delightful to me,' said Rinconete, 'and I should like to be of some use to such an excellent brotherhood.'

'Heaven always favours good desires,' said Monipodio.

As they were talking, a knock came at the door, Monipodio went out to see who it was, and the answer came:

'Open up, Mr Monipodio; it's Repolido.'

Cariharta heard him, and screamed at the top of her voice,

'Don't answer, Mr Monipodio, don't open to that sailor from Tarpeia, that tiger of Ocaña.'

Monipodio opened the door to Repolido in spite of all this; but when Cariharta saw that he was letting him in, she ran to the room where the bucklers were and, shutting the door behind her, she shouted from inside,

'Take this good-for-nothing away, this murderer of innocents, this frightener of tame doves.'

Maniferro and Chiquiznaque were holding Repolido, who was determined to get in to where Cariharta was; but as they didn't let him, he called from outside, 'Don't be angry any more; come down for goodness' sake, if you want to be married!'

'Married, you wretch?' answered Cariharta. 'That's a fine tune to play. You may want to marry me, but I'd rather marry a skeleton than you!'

'Come on, you stupid girl!' replied Repolido; 'let's stop this, for it's getting late. Don't get on your high horse because I'm talking to you so meekly and behaving so humbly, because, God knows, if my anger gets the better of me, the second attack may be worse than the first. Give in, let's eat our humble pie, and not give it all to the devil!'

'The devil can do what he likes with you,' said Cariharta, 'as long as I never see you again.'

'What did I say?' said Repolido, 'I'm beginning to think, Miss Strumpet, that I'm going to have to put a stop to this, whatever the consequences.'

At this Monipodio said, 'There must be no insolence in my presence. Cariharta will come out, not because of your threats, but out of regard for me, and everything must be done properly; for quarrels between persons who are fond of each other make it all the sweeter when they make up. Oh Juliana! Oh, my girl!

Oh my Cariharta! Come out here, for my sake, and I'll make Repolido beg you for pardon on his knees.'

'If he does that,' said Escalanta, 'we'll all be on his side and beg Juliana to come out.'

'If I have to give in at the cost ot my dignity,' said Repolido, 'I won't surrender to a bunch of ragamuffins; but if it's because Cariharta wishes it, I won't just kneel, but I'll be a slave and put a nail in my forehead for her sake.'

Chiquiznaque and Maniferro laughed at this, at which Repolido got so angry, thinking that they were making fun of him, that he said, looking absolutely furious, 'If anyone laughs or thinks of laughing at what Cariharta has said, or may say, about me, or I about her, I say he lies and will be lying every time he laughs or thinks of laughing.'

Chiquiznaque and Maniferro gave each other such a look that Monipodio realized that the whole thing would come to a nasty end unless he came to the rescue, and so placing himself straight away between them, he said,

'Don't go on, gentlemen, let's have no more threats; swallow your words, and since they don't amount to very much, don't let anyone take them to heart.'

'We are quite sure,' answered Chiquiznaque, 'that this sort of warning has never been given or will be given on our account, for if anyone thought it was, the tambourine is in the hands of someone who knows how to play it.'

'We've got a tambourine here too, Mr Chiquiznaque,' replied Repolido, 'and if necessary we can play the bells as well. As I've just said, anyone who pokes fun is a liar; and if anyone thinks differently, let him follow me, for I'll cut him down to size with my sword, and that's that.'

And saying this, he made for the door.

Cariharta was listening to this, and when she realized that he was going off in a huff, she rushed out, saying, 'Stop him, don't let him go, or he'll be up to his pranks. Can't you see that he's annoyed? And he's a real Judas Maccabeus when it comes to being tough. Come here, my hero, you apple of my eye.'

And closing in on him, she clutched him firmly by his cloak, and with the help of Monipodio, who came up, they stopped him. Chiquiznaque and Maniferro didn't know whether to be angry or not, so they stopped where they were, waiting to see what Repolido would do. When he saw Cariharta and Monipodio appealing to him, he turned round and said,

'Friends should never upset friends or make fun of friends, especially when they see that friends are upset.'

'There's no friend here,' answered Maniferro, 'who wants to upset or make fun of any friend, and since we are all friends let us shake hands like friends.'

Whereupon Monipodio replied, 'You have all spoken like good friends, and being friends you must shake hands like friends.'

So they shook hands, and Escalanta, taking off one of her shoes, began to beat on it like a drum. Then Gananciosa took a new palm broom, which happened to be there, and scraping it made a noise which, although rough and harsh, harmonized with the music of the shoe. Monipodio broke a plate and made two clappers, which, placed between his fingers and clicked together at great speed, kept in tune with the shoe and the broom.

Rinconete and Cortadillo were amazed at the idea of the broom because until then they had never seen it. Maniferro noticed this, and said to them,

'Are you surprised at the broom? Well no wonder, because you couldn't find a cheaper and easier way of making music. Indeed I heard a student say the other day that not even Norpheus, who pulled his wife out of hell, nor Marion, who rode on a dolphin and came out of the sea as if she were riding on a hired mule, nor that other great musician who made a city which had a hundred doors and as many posterns, ever invented a better sort of music, so easy to learn, so simple to play, so free of frets, pegs and strings, and with no need of tuning. And what's more I swear they say it was invented by a fellow from this city, who prides himself on being a real Hector where music is concerned.'

'That I can well believe,' answered Rinconete, 'but let's listen to what our musicians want to sing; for you notice that Gananciosa has cleared her throat, which is a sign that she wants to sing.'

And this was true, because Monipodio had asked her to sing some *seguidillas* which were in fashion at the time; but it was Escalanta who started first, and with a thin, quavery voice she sang as follows:

> A sandy-haired lad from Seville
> has stolen my heart and my will.

Gananciosa went on to sing:

> To a dark handsome boy with green eyes
> every girl who has spirit will rise.

And then Monipodio, shaking the clappers at great speed, said:

> When lovers who quarrel make peace,
> past furies their pleasures increase.

Cariharta did not want her pleasure to be passed over in silence, so, picking up another shoe, she started to dance, and accompanied the others with the words:

> Stop beating me, for you must see,
> you hurt your own flesh, striking me.

'Sing something straightforward,' said Repolido at this point, 'and don't bother with past history, for there's no sense in that; let bygones be bygones, let's make a new start, and let it go at that.'

It looked as if the singing was not likely to end for some time, but suddenly there came a quick knock at the door. Monipodio went out to see who it was, and the guard told him that the Justice of the Peace had appeared at the end of the street, preceded by two constables, Tordillo and Cercnícalo. The people inside heard what was happening, and they all got so excited that Cariharta and Escalanta put their shoes on the wrong way round. Gananciosa left her broom, Monipodio his clappers, and the music gave way to an uneasy silence. Chiquiznaque didn't open his mouth, Repolido was stunned and Maniferro was struck dumb. All of them, some in one direction and some in another, disappeared, going up to the rooftops to get away and escape over them to the next street. An unexpected gunshot or a sudden clap of thunder never frightened a flock of doves caught unawares more thoroughly than the news of the arrival of the Justice of the Peace scared and threw into confusion that gathering of good people. The two novices Rinconete and Cortadillo did not know what to do, and stood still, waiting to see the outcome of that sudden storm. In fact the guard came back to say that the Justice had gone by without stopping, giving no sign or trace of any suspicion.

And as he was telling Monipodio this, a young gentleman

came to the door dressed, as they say, like a man about town. Monipodio brought him in with him, and ordered Chiquiznaque, Maniferro and Repolido to be called, and no one else. As Rinconete and Cortadillo had stayed in the courtyard, they could hear all the conversation that Monipodio had with the newcomer, who asked Monipodio why his orders had been so badly carried out. Monipodio answered that he didn't even know what had been done, but that the official in charge of the job was there, and that he would give a very good account of himself. At this point Chiquiznaque came down and Monipodio asked him if he had carried out the fourteen-wound knifing job he had been charged with.

'Which one?' asked Chiquiznaque. 'Do you mean the one on that merchant at the crossroads?'

'That's the one,' said the gentleman.

'Well, what happened,' answered Chiquiznaque, 'was that I waited for him last night at the door of his house, and he came before prayer-time. I went up to him, had a good look at his face, and realized that it was so small that it was absolutely impossible to fit fourteen knife wounds into it; and finding that I couldn't carry out my promise and do what was contained in my destructions . . .'

'"Instructions" you must mean,' said the gentleman, 'not "destructions".'

'That's what I meant,' answered Chiquiznaque. 'I say that as the wounds wouldn't fit into the small space available, so as not to waste my journey I knifed a lackey of his, and with the best quality wounds.'

'I'd rather,' said the gentleman, 'that you'd given the master seven slashes than the servant fourteen. In fact, you haven't carried out my orders properly, but no matter; I shan't miss the thirty ducats I left by way of deposit. I'll bid you gentlemen farewell.'

And saying this, he took off his hat and turned round to go away, but Monipodio caught hold of the tweed cloak he was wearing and said to him,

'You stay here and keep your promise, for we have kept ours very honourably and to the best advantage; you owe us twenty ducats, and you won't leave here until you've given them to me, or some security worth the same amount.'

'Is this what you call keeping your promise?' answered the gentleman; 'knifing the servant instead of the master?'

'You're all at sea, sir,' said Chiquiznaque. 'You don't seem to remember that proverb which says, "Love me, love my dog!"'

'How does that proverb fit in here?' replied the gentleman.

'Well, isn't it all the same,' went on Chiquiznaque, 'to say: "hate me, hate my dog"? So the merchant is the master, you hate him; the servant is the dog, and by hitting the dog you hit his master and the debt is settled and properly discharged. So all there is to do is to pay up straight away without further ado.'

'I'll swear to that,' added Monipodio; 'and you've taken the words right out of my mouth, friend Chiquiznaque. And so, my fine sir, don't you get mixed up in punctilios with your servants and friends, but take my advice and pay straight away for the work that's been done; and if you want the master to have another knifing, according to the number of slashes his face can carry, I can assure you that it's as good as done.'

'If that's the case,' answered the young man, 'I shall be very willing and happy to pay for both in full.'

'Have no more doubt about this,' said Monipodio, 'than about being a Christian; for Chiquiznaque will give him a knifing that fits him as if he were born with it.'

'Well, with this assurance and promise,' answered the gentleman, 'take this chain as security for the twenty ducats owing and for forty which I'm prepared to pay for the knifing we've agreed on. It weighs a thousand *reales*, and you might as well keep it, because I have an idea that another fourteen slashes will be required before long.'

With this he took a chain from his neck, and gave it to Monipodio, who from its colour and weight saw clearly that it was no fake. Monipodio received it with every sign of pleasure and politeness, like the most well-bred man alive. Chiquiznaque was charged with the execution of the deed, and undertook to do it that night. The gentleman went off quite satisfied, and then Monipodio called all the others, who had gone off in a fright. They all came down and Monipodio, standing in the middle, took out a notebook which he had in the hood of his cloak, and gave it to Rinconete to read, because he could not read himself. Rinconete opened it, and on the first page he saw that it said:

List of knifings for this week
The first, to the merchant at the crossroads; price fifty crowns. Received thirty on account. Executor, Chiquiznaque.

'I don't think there are any more, my boy,' said Monipodio. 'Go on and look under "List of beatings".'

Rinconete turned over, and saw on another page: *List of beatings*. And underneath it said:

To the man who keeps the chop-house in Alfalfa: twelve top-quality strokes, at a crown a piece. Eight given on account. Time limit six days. Executor, Maniferro.

'You could cross that item off,' said Maniferro, 'for I'll have it done tonight.'

'Any more, my boy?' said Monipodio.

'Yes, there is another,' answered Rinconete, 'and it says this:

To the hump-backed tailor known for his sins as Silguero, six strokes of the best, at the request of the lady who left the necklace. Executor, Desmochado.'

'I'm amazed,' said Monipodio, 'that this item is still on the books. Desmochado must be out of action, for it's two days after the time limit and he hasn't been anywhere near the job.'

'I met him yesterday,' said Maniferro, 'and he told me that because the hump-back had been laid up ill he hadn't carried it out.'

'I'm prepared to believe that,' said Monipodio, 'because I consider Desmochado to be so good at his job, that if it weren't for such a good reason he would have done even greater things. Any more, lad?'

'No, sir,' answered Rinconete.

'Then go on,' said Monipodio, 'and look where it says "List of miscellaneous offences".'

Rinconete went on, and on another page he found this:

List of miscellaneous offences
Namely, ink-throwings, juniper-oil smearings, fixing of *sambenitos* and horns, practical jokes, frights, and disturbances, threatened stabbings, publication of libels, etc.

'What does it say underneath?' asked Monipodio.

'It says: "Smearing with oil at the house . . ."'

'Don't say which house, because I know where it is,' answered Monipodio, 'and I am the *sine qua non* and executor of this bit of nonsense, and there are four crowns paid on account, and the total charge is eight.'

'That's true,' said Rinconete, 'for all this is written down here, and lower down it says: "Fixing of horns".'

'Don't read the name of the house nor where it is,' said Monipodio; 'for it's bad enough that the injury should be done, without its being published abroad, for it is a great load on one's conscience. At least, I'd rather fix a hundred horns and as many *sambenitos*, provided I'm paid for my work, than mention it once, even to the mother who bore me.'

'The executor of this is Narigueta,' said Rinconete.

'That's already done and paid for,' said Monipodio. 'See if there are any more, for if I remember rightly, there should be a twenty-crown fright, half paid for, and the executor is the whole community, and the time limit the end of this month; if it's carried out to the letter, without missing a jot, it will be one of the best things that have happened in this city for a long time. Give me the book, young man, for I know there aren't any more, and I know too that business is very slack. But there are better times ahead and we'll have more to do than we want, for not a leaf falls without God's will, and it's not our business to force anyone to take his revenge. Anyway, everyone wants to do his own dirty work and no one wants to pay the cost of work which he can do himself.'

'That's it,' said Repolido in reply. 'But hurry up and give us our orders, Mr Monipodio, for it's getting late and the heat's coming up fast.'

'What you have to do,' answered Monipodio, 'is to go to your posts, all of you, and not to leave them until Sunday, when we'll all meet here and have a share-out of anything that's come our way, without doing injury to anyone. Rinconete the Good and Cortadillo will have as their beat until Sunday from the Torre de Oro, outside the city, to the Alcázar gate, where they can sit on a bench and do their tricks. For I've seen others less clever than they getting away every day with more than twenty *reales* in small change, not to mention silver, with a single pack of cards, and with four cards missing at that. Ganchuelo will show you the beat; and it doesn't matter much if you go up to San Sebastián and San Telmo, although it's only right and proper that no one should encroach on someone else's territory.'

The two of them kissed his hand for the kindnesses done to them, and promised him to carry out their duty faithfully and well, with all diligence and caution.

Whereupon Monipodio took from the hood of his cloak a paper, on which was a list of the members of the brotherhood, and he told Rinconete to put his and Cortadillo's names on it; but as there was no inkpot he gave him the paper to take away and get it written at the first apothecary's, putting 'Rinconete and Cortadillo, members; probation, none; Rinconete, card sharper; Cortadillo, pickpocket'; and the day, month, and year, not mentioning parents or birthplace. As they were dealing with this, one of the old 'hornets' came in and said,

'I've come to tell you that I've just this minute met Lobillo from Málaga at the Gradas and he tells me that he's so much improved in his work that he can take money off the devil himself if he only has clean cards; and that because he's been beaten up he's not coming to register and swear the customary oath of allegiance at the moment; but that on Sunday he'll be here without fail.'

'I was always convinced,' said Monipodio, 'that this Lobillo must be without equal in his craft, because he has the best hands for it that you could wish for; for to be a good tradesman in one's profession, one needs good instruments to practise it just as much as intelligence to learn it.'

'I also came across Judío,' said the old man, 'in a lodging house in the calle de Tintores. He was wearing clerical dress, and had gone to stay there because he had been told that two wealthy Peruvians live in the same house. He wanted to see if he could get a game with them, even if only for small stakes, because it might lead to something big. He says that he will be at the meeting on Sunday too, and will give account of himself.'

'Judío is a great thief too,' said Monipodio, 'and knows what he's up to. It's days since I've seen him, and he's not behaving right. Indeed if he doesn't mend his ways I'll break his head; for he's no more in orders than the Grand Turk, and knows no more Latin than my mother. Is there any other news?'

'No,' said the old man, 'at least as far as I know.'

'Well, all right,' said Monipodio. 'Take this trifle' – and he distributed about forty *reales* among them – 'and don't let anyone fail to appear on Sunday, for there'll be a proper reckoning up.'

They all thanked him; Repolido and Cariharta embraced each other again, and so did Escalanta and Maniferro and Gananciosa and Chiquiznaque, agreeing that that night, after they had finished work at the house, they would see each other in Pipota's house, where Monipodio said he would also be going to inspect the laundry basket. Then he would have to go and do the oiling job and cross it off the books. He embraced Rinconete and Cortadillo and, giving them his blessing, dismissed them, charging them never to have any settled and fixed lodging, for the sake of everyone's safety. Ganchuelo went with them to show them their beat, reminding them not to fail to appear on Sunday, because, he believed, Monipodio was going to give them an important lecture on matters concerning their craft. With this he went off, leaving the two comrades amazed at what they had seen.

Rinconete, although only a boy, was very intelligent and good-natured. As he had accompanied his father in the business of selling bulls, he knew something about the proper way to speak, and he was highly amused when he thought of the words which he had heard Monipodio and the others of that blessed community say, especially when for '*per modum sufragii . . .*' he had said 'by way of outrage'; and 'stupend' for 'stipend', when referring to their winnings; and when Cariharta said that Repolido was like a 'sailor of Tarpeia and a tiger of Ocaña', when she meant 'Hircania'; with a thousand and one other absurdities like or even worse than these. He was especially amused when she said that heaven would offset against her sins the labour she had put into gaining the twenty-four *reales*. He was also amazed by the assurance they had and their confidence that they would go to heaven because they didn't fail to perform their devotions, when they were up to their eyes in stealing and murder and offences against God. And he laughed at the good old woman, Pipota, who left the stolen laundry basket safely in her house and went off to put wax candles in front of the images, and thought that by doing that she would go to heaven all dressed and shod. He was no less astounded by the obedience and respect they all felt for Monipodio, when he was such a barbarous, uncouth and soulless wretch. He thought of what he had read in the memorandum book and the practices in which they were all engaged. Finally, he was shocked by the slackness of the law in that famous city of Seville, where such pernicious and perverted people could live almost openly; and he made up his mind to advise his companion that they should not spend much time in that evil and abandoned way of life, so uncertain, lawless and dissolute. But all the same, carried away by his youth and lack of experience, he spent some months longer with the community, during which things happened to him which require more time than this to tell; and so the account of their life and marvellous doings is left for another occasion, with those of their master Monipodio and the other events which took place in that infamous academy, all worth consideration and capable of serving as an example and warning to those who may read them.

READ MORE IN PENGUIN

For complete information about books available from Penguin and how to order them, please write to us at the appropriate address below. Please note that for copyright reasons the selection of books varies from country to country.

IN THE UNITED KINGDOM: Please write to *Dept. EP, Penguin Books Ltd, Bath Road, Harmondsworth, Middlesex UB7 0DA.*

IN THE UNITED STATES: Please write to *Consumer Sales, Penguin USA, P.O. Box 999, Dept. 17109, Bergenfield, New Jersey 07621-0120.* VISA and MasterCard holders call 1-800-253-6476 to order Penguin titles.

IN CANADA: Please write to *Penguin Books Canada Ltd, 10 Alcorn Avenue, Suite 300, Toronto, Ontario M4V 3B2.*

IN AUSTRALIA: Please write to *Penguin Books Australia Ltd, P.O. Box 257, Ringwood, Victoria 3134.*

IN NEW ZEALAND: Please write to *Penguin Books (NZ) Ltd, Private Bag 102902, North Shore Mail Centre, Auckland 10.*

IN INDIA: Please write to *Penguin Books India Pvt Ltd, 706 Eros Apartments, 56 Nehru Place, New Delhi 110 019.*

IN THE NETHERLANDS: Please write to *Penguin Books Netherlands bv, Postbus 3507, NL-1001 AH Amsterdam.*

IN GERMANY: Please write to *Penguin Books Deutschland GmbH, Metzlerstrasse 26, 60594 Frankfurt am Main.*

IN SPAIN: Please write to *Penguin Books S. A., Bravo Murillo 19, 1° B, 28015 Madrid.*

IN ITALY: Please write to *Penguin Italia s.r.l., Via Felice Casati 20, I-20124 Milano.*

IN FRANCE: Please write to *Penguin France S. A., 17 rue Lejeune, F-31000 Toulouse.*

IN JAPAN: Please write to *Penguin Books Japan, Ishikiribashi Building, 2-5-4, Suido, Bunkyo-ku, Tokyo 112.*

IN GREECE: Please write to *Penguin Hellas Ltd, Dimocritou 3, GR-106 71 Athens.*

IN SOUTH AFRICA: Please write to *Longman Penguin Southern Africa (Pty) Ltd, Private Bag X08, Bertsham 2013.*